SHORELINE OF INFINITY

Aw...
fict...
in S...
Uni...

 **WORLDCON GLASGOW 2024**

ISSUE 38:
SUMMER 2024

ISSN: 2059-2590
ISBN: 978-1-7395359-2-6

© 2024 *Shoreline of Infinity*
Contributors retain copyright of own work

Submissions of fiction, art, reviews, poetry, non-fiction are welcomed: visit the website to find out how to submit

www.shorelineofinfinity.com

Publisher
Shoreline of Infinity Publications /
The New Curiosity Shop
Edinburgh
Scotland

180724

Co-founders:
Noel Chidwick,
Mark Toner

The Brilliant Editorial Team:

Fiction Editor:
Eris Young

Reviews Editor:
Ann Landmann

Non-fiction Editor:
Pippa Goldschmidt

Production Editors:
Noel Chidwick,
Andrew Lindsay

Copy-editors:
Pippa Goldschmidt
Iain Maloney
Eris Young
Cat Hellisen

EDITORIAL TEAM

CONTENTS

1	Pull up a Log
3	Scars
	David McGillveray
19	Intersections of the Species
	Andrew Kozma
31	Transference
	LeeAnn Perry
39	Degrees of Freedom
	Tim Major
48	When I Get Younger
	Dylan Kwok
55	Sunriders
	Anna Ziemons-McLean
71	Seed
	M. A. R. Rinaldi
89	Forgetting is Their Word for Death
	Paul McQuade
98	Noise and Sparks
	Ruth EJ Booth
104	Science Fiction and Abolishing the Police
	S. J. Groenewegen
108	Bram E. Gieben
	Q& A with Pippa Goldschmidt
112	Multiverse
	Anna Cheung
115	Time Cleaves Itself
	Jeda Pearl
118	Reviews
	Umbilical by Teika Marija Smits
	The Darkest Timeline by Bram E. Gieben
	Mal Goes To War by Edward Ashton
127	Wanted: SF stories by Scottish Writers
128	Star Draws
	Mark Toner

COVER ART
Siobhan Mcdonald

Little Airship:
Becca McCall

FIRST CONTACT
www.shorelineofinfinity.com
contact@shorelineofinfinity.com
Twitter: @shoreinf
Also on Instagram & Bluesky

PULL UP A LOG

Shoreline of Infinity welcomes everyone who has travelled from around the planet to Scotland and to Worldcon, Glasgow 2024.

We stand to applaud the amazing team behind Worldcon 2024, who have worked long hours over the last few years to make it happen: their enthusiasm and dedication is an example to us all.

That thousands of people, who share their love of science fiction have gathered together, shows the power of imagination, and the spirit of human beings to embrace story, and ideas. The Olympics may celebrate the achievements of the human body, but we cheer for the strength of creativity inside every one of us. Every spark, every flame.

Shoreline of Infinity began ten years ago with the hope that we could create a space where science fiction writers could entertain and inform us – and we wanted to help bring that spark to life, giving oxygen to new and emerging writers.

We're thirty-eight issues in and we can say we have done our bit: we have published writers from every continent. If you are one of those travellers to Worldcon, come and say hello to us in the Dealers' Hall.

—Noel Chidwick
Co-founder, Editor-in-Chief
Shoreline of Infinity

The cover of Shoreline of Infinity 1 by Bill Wright illustrates our thoughts: no matter where you come from or who you are, you are welcome to join us around the flames and share our dreams.

Scars

David McGillveray

Two hundred human ships hung in formation above the green shoulder of Jal. They faced an armada of spheres, thousands of them, dancing in erratic orbits about one another, expanding and contracting, merging and separating. Thin fingers of communication reached between the fleets, tentative and suspicious, while below the planet was laid out like a game board.

※

The equatorial forest girdled the world, a vast belt stretching all the way to the cold zones at the poles, broken only by the reflection of sunlight on open water and the spines of mountain chains. We had travelled three hours north from Verwah in the southern hemisphere, the hull of the gelcar transparent so it seemed there was only the lilac sky and the forest, and that I was one of the flying things that glided above the canopy. Jal was a prize and we were giving it away.

"Eight minutes," announced the gelcar's subintelligence. I prepared myself, running through the series of mental exercises that calmed and sharpened. When I opened my eyes again, the vehicle was curving towards a brown scar among the trees, the site of the temporary border post.

I stole a glance at my companion. Miriam Tudu wasn't much of a conversationalist for a professional communicator. The Translator had not said a word for the entire journey; hood pulled forward over her bowed head, ankles crossed and hands in lap. Rings on her fingers held big faceted stones denoting her progression through the categories of her order. There were perhaps thirty individuals in all of the human sphere who could claim the right to wear the circular brown gemstone on the middle finger of her right hand, the one that signalled she was a Speaker to the Huul.

"You are ready?" I asked her.

"Yes, Nama." A deep voice, rising from the depths of her barrel of a torso.

The transport descended and its keel became opaque, cutting off my view of the collection of short-term structures behind their security fence.

The subintelligence informed us we were free to undo our restraints. My knees ached from all the sitting, my head from the thinking and the worrying. The gelcar's skin split open and I was hit by the heat and the smell of the forest, an assault of life and earth and decay. My undersuit struggled to adjust as it sought to regulate my body's temperature.

I knew Master Halder, the officer who greeted us, from the exhaustive planning sessions for the handover. I'm sure the Huul Mothers would have been outraged to hear a male had played such a significant role in its arrangement.

He dipped his head. "Nama Giri. After so many virtuals it's a pleasure to meet you in the flesh."

I smiled. "Likewise, Master." He was shorter, more muscular in person. He sweated under a rather silly purple dress beret. "Is everything arranged with the Huul?"

"I'm proceeding under that assumption, Nama." He flicked his eyes towards Translator Tudu. She cut an incongruous figure in her robes, almost as wide as she was tall, hiding in the shadow of her hood.

"They're capricious bitches, the Mothers," I said. "They like to play games."

"Indeed. Shall we walk through the final briefing? There's tea." Halder gestured towards a dome set some distance from the landing pad, its reflective surface rippling in the hot air.

The history of human/Huul contact had been a series of traps designed to give the Huul the maximum opportunity to take offence. They regarded all dialogue with "undercreatures" as a diminution almost too much to bear. Any interaction with males of any species was viewed with a disgust bordering on mania. No significant discussions were allowed to take place using technological means. They would communicate only in their own language, and it had to be perfectly enunciated.

They looked for insult so keenly they barely listened to what was actually being said. Still, I knew a few humans with plenty of the same traits.

"They're using Proxies on Jal," I remarked.

"I hope that means the Huul wish for success. What dialogue we've had in the past has been so much more effective with them involved." Halder sat opposite me and prepared the tea meticulously. He'd had real porcelain brought all the way up here, I noted with appreciation.

"They'd be crazy not to want this concluded peacefully. The treaty has successfully halted the expansion of the human sphere right here." I sipped from the delicate cup Halder presented me with. "The Hybrid Council must have been particularly distracted the day this was agreed to. If the Huul had a sense of humour, they'd be laughing their gigantic arses off."

"You don't support the treaty?"

"Do *you?*" I shrugged, putting my cup down. "It puts off the war. But that doesn't mean it's not still coming."

Miriam Tudu sat silently by my side, her tea untouched, face in shadow.

"What do you think, Translator?" I asked her.

"I think it is always best to communicate," she said after a long moment. "May I excuse myself? I wish to practice my phrasings." Without waiting for me to answer she stood and left us.

"She's spent time on several worlds with the Proxies, I believe," Halder remarked, embarrassed, "with the few allowed to interact with humans. Her record is impressive."

"Yes, she appears the best choice, and charming with it."

We drank tea. In time, he pressed a finger to his ear. "It's happening."

✻

A path hacked through the trees formed a tunnel within the dense forest. Squeals and thrashings emanated from the jungle, from protagonists unseen, and the mulch gave beneath my boots as we walked. Halder led while I trudged along with Tudu beside me, a phalanx of troopers and their accompanying drones at our backs.

I felt oppressed by the engulfing vegetation, concerned about how events would transpire and for my own performance, although in truth I was to be little more than a passive witness as sole rights to Jal were handed to the Huul. Again, I passed myself through the calming mental exercises my tutors had taught me all those years ago.

The unnamed river, known only by its map reference, had been agreed by both sides as a boundary between our respective territories. It was a border sitting upon a greater border, in a system where the human and Huul domains ground against one another.

"This is where we leave you, Nama," Master Halder announced. I could see a faint window of sunlight ahead. He took my hand

and kissed it, surprising me with the emotion in his voice. "I wish you success, all of us do."

"Thank you, Master," I replied.

He smiled, nodded to Tudu and led his troopers away, leaving us with a solitary light-globe floating like a tiny sun in the darkness.

"Just us girls now," I said.

In answer, the Translator reached up and pulled the hood from her head for the first time since we had left Verwah, rings flashing.

She looked so much more alien in this setting. The lamplight reflected in the great black pool of the listening eye that filled the centre of her forehead, unblinking. Faint lines from the many surgeries that had made her what she was crisscrossed her bald skull. Her human features were crushed into the lower half of her face, piggy eyes over a flattened nose, a cut of a mouth above a chinless jaw.

"The Proxy will be waiting," she said.

We headed towards the point of daylight ahead of us. Sweat prickled my forehead, as much from nerves as the pressing heat. The jungle had grown quiet and I could hear water.

The lamp retreated back up the tunnel and we emerged blinking by the river, an opaque brown tumult rushing between high banks, its surface broken by endlessly reforming eddies that reminded me of the dance of the Huul fleet. A breeze brought relief after the forest path.

Eighty metres across the water stood the Huul delegation – an enormous Proxy and its smaller companion. I had never seen these creatures outside of sims. The lead Proxy sat back on its rearmost legs, opening the rest to reveal an eggshell blue underside. Points of light flared on its belly, flashing at random points and with differing intensities and durations, like the blinking of some ancient calculating machine.

"What's it saying?" I asked Tudu, but she held up her hand as the Proxy's light-speech continued.

"Formal introductions," the Translator hissed when the Proxy ceased its signalling. "Identification protocols. I must respond."

Before I could ask more, Tudu shed her robe to stand naked beside me. I couldn't help but stare despite all my preparation and felt a surge of emotion I couldn't quite put a name to: sympathy, revulsion, awe?

Uncovered, the Translator's body was a slab of pale flesh, unnaturally wide and long, like a biological screen supported by short, muscular legs. Her human eyes were screwed shut in concentration beneath the hypnotic depths of her listening eye, the organ that allowed her to draw meaning from the frequencies and intervals of Huul light-speech. Sparks of light blazed from the series of glands grafted to her torso. The heat coming off her, was fierce enough for me to take a step back, and I wondered what toll the process took on her.

A few answering signals flashed from across the river and then Tudu stooped to pull the robe back around her shoulders. She shook herself and gave me a defiant look, as if daring me to feel anything for her.

I didn't rise to it. "Well?" I demanded.

"The Proxy is designated Nine for the duration of this interaction. We're to get in the cradle." Tudu produced a flask and sucked greedily at its spigot.

"What?" I asked stupidly and then noticed the thing being pulled across the river towards us on a line by the smaller of the two aliens, using a simple pulley as old as civilisation. We were to be ferried across like sacks of vegetables! "You're kidding me." I looked at my companion. "You're not."

The cradle thumped into the riverbank a short distance from where we stood. I looked at it in distaste, sighed and helped Tudu climb inside. No sooner were we settled than we were jerked back into motion, swaying a few metres above the swirling brown water.

"What else was said?" We sat opposite each other in the cramped cradle. It was difficult not to stare into Tudu's listening eye, to become lost in it.

"I described our credentials and explained your status as senior human representative," Tudu explained. "The Proxy is to conduct us into the presence of the Huul Mother as agreed. The Mother is a member of their First Family. It is an encouraging sign."

I nodded. "Anything else?"

"The other creature is a male slave animal. When we get to the other side do not acknowledge it. This will insult the Proxy, and hence the Huul Mother herself. Remember at all times the Proxy is an avatar for the Mother. It has no status of its own, it is used simply as a vessel. We must regard it as if we are communicating directly with the Huul herself."

"But we're not, are we? The Huul isn't directly controlling her Proxy."

"No, she is interpreting the Mother's wishes. I trained with Nine's kin on the world Endemionada, after I was first forged into a Translator. They are fully independent sentients, sensitive and intuitive in their way. But the Huul require we regard them otherwise. To them, their Proxies are just automata."

As we drew closer the Proxy's sheer size became more evident. Roughly arachnoid, it had risen from its speaking stance to stand on eight powerful legs, the spikes of its pincer feet stabbed into the soil. Additional manipulatory appendages were arranged around the edge of its carapace, waving like fronds in water. The bone grey chitin that armoured it was whorled with intricate patterns, like cyclones roaming a world's atmosphere. It regarded us from two enormous blue compound eyes set like clusters of sapphires on either side of a wide shovel-like head held four metres above the ground. I felt the mass and power of it before I caught its scent, an acid musk that burned the back of my throat like inhaling from a pan of frying chillies.

The cage bumped against the far bank and we scrambled gracelessly out of the contraption. The Proxy could have torn us apart like dolls, and I thought how vulnerable I had allowed myself to be made here, disconnected and unprotected. A netstream link and a good, heavy pistol would have made me feel a whole lot better.

Tudu disrobed again and I stepped aside to let her speak. Again, I felt the heat of her words as the specialized glands flared in the sequences of the Huul language. The Proxy sank back into its own speaking posture, exposing its belly, and it struck me that it made itself vulnerable when it spoke. Perhaps the Mothers had contrived things that way.

The Proxy's underside was not the smooth, pale surface I had presumed from the other side of the river, but a mutilated landscape of scarred flesh, pitted and pocked and tracked with the lines of ragged incisions where awful blades must have cut. A feeding mouth sat amongst the damage, surrounded by a beard of short tentacles – a pink maw that opened and closed uncontrollably as the light-speech burned in its body. I thought of our own Translator's marks, and how both of them had been cut in order to allow this communication. At least on the human side our Translators were volunteers.

Tudu turned to me when they were done. "Nine requests our forgiveness and informs us we must journey further to where the gracious Mother awaits. All is prepared for our supplication."

"Supplication!" I spluttered. "This is a mutually agreed contract between our two spheres!"

Tudu, once again covered by her robes, said, "Perhaps I misinterpreted a nuance in Nine's words."

I stared at her, irate. "I bloody doubt it."

Tudu failed to look sheepish. "There are some final checks."

"What now?"

The Proxy moved towards us quickly. It brandished a thing the size of a human baby, soft and grey and slimy like an oyster. I drew back instinctively, realizing that only the river was at my back.

"Be still," Tudu barked. "It's a scanning device. Technological artefacts above a certain specification are forbidden."

The Proxy waved the thing above our heads and around our bodies. Apparently satisfied, it retreated before pushing the device into its feeding mouth and swallowing it whole. I became aware that I was gaping.

Our host was already moving off, leaving the male slave by the river, hopefully to attend to our return journey. The great flattened shell of its body and armoured limbs pushed easily through the jungle. We followed in its wake and its stink.

※

As we emerged from the tree line I was reminded again of what a treasure we were losing here. I stood with Tudu and Nine at the top of a long, gentle slope that fell away for kilometres beneath my feet, carpeted with grass and sprays of pink, yellow and vanilla wildflowers. The perfumed air was filled with the hum of insect life and the fluttering of tiny pollinators. After the heat and shadow beneath the trees, the sun lit my face and a part of me wanted to lie on my tummy and roll down the hill like a little girl.

"The meeting place lies down the valley, Nama," Tudu told me.

I nodded as we started off again, trying to enjoy my surroundings, but I soon sank inwards. It was a trait of mine that all the meditation and mind-tricks had never quite managed to expunge.

Wherever humans and Huul had encountered one another there had been friction. Human settlements and assets had been plundered and devastated all along the line of contact and then met with denials as insulting as they were flimsy. The destruction of an orbital ring in the Orulus system cost a hundred thousand lives. As we discovered more about our new rivals, we learned how they denuded worlds of resources, consuming what they could and destroying what they could not. Indigenous races, like the Proxy's, were enslaved or exterminated.

There was nothing in the Huul's history or our AIs' behavioural models that suggested any détente could be anything more than an interval. It was only the Huul's fear of human technology and the self-delusion of our own leadership that had made this treaty possible at all. Yes, it was historic, but it was an accommodation that history would reveal as a great mistake. I was sure of it.

So here I was, reaching out my hand to have it bitten. The Hybrid Council, that finely balanced mix of human and AI planners, were teaching this unbeliever a lesson in humility and duty.

"You think Jal is beautiful," Tudu surprised me, interrupting my thoughts.

"Yes. Don't you agree?"

The Translator held her hands clasped before her as she walked, like some penitent. The rings on her fingers shone in the sunlight. "My other senses are dulled. I find beauty elsewhere, in the patterns of language. But that is not my point. The Huul desire this planet greatly, though not for its meadows and sunsets, and they always take what they want. The hydrocarbon seeps are like a drug to them."

Ahead and below, a string of linked, inky lagoons filled the valley floor. The way became steeper and in places we had to proceed cautiously, loose soil shifting beneath our boots as we made our way beside sandy stone ridges striated with layers of darker material. The lushness of the vegetation higher up gave way to scrub and thorn, where odd, many-armed Jalan cacti reached for the lilac sky. Our guide carried on relentlessly, balanced on its many limbs, unspeaking.

As we descended deeper into what was rapidly becoming a broad-bottomed gorge, I caught the chemical funk of the lakes for the first time. I thought of tar pools and bitumen, of newly laid roads and industrial installations. Our first surveys of Jal had detected extensive basins of hydrocarbons close to the surface, where pressure from below caused oil and gas to seep to the surface, creating vast swamps and leaching into sands and waterways. These held no energy value for either us or the Huul but they led to a particular set of geological characteristics our rivals had a peculiar affinity for, leading to much speculation about their biology and origins. In short, the horrible mollusks loved a petroleum bath.

I could see no technological signs of the Huul's presence other than the movement of their Proxies in the vicinity of the first lake. I didn't doubt, though, that our progress was watched by hundreds of eyes hanging in orbit.

The first and largest of the lakes was perhaps a kilometre across and twice as long, its still surface obscured in places by strange fogs that split the sunlight into rainbow colours before dispersing and reforming elsewhere. The tang of crude oil was almost overpowering and I pulled up the mask of my undersuit. As we approached the shore, I saw a troop of eight Proxies making their way around the lakeside on some unknowable errand for their mistresses. Others stood alone and sentinel-like. I was struck by the silence, of the water, of the Proxies. I could hear my own breathing inside the mask, our footsteps in the sand. The Huul Mother remained unseen.

I forced myself to speak. "What now?" I looked up at the Proxy towering above our heads. "Where's your boss, Proxy?"

Tudu placed a hand lightly on my forearm. "Patience, Nama. A place is prepared."

Nine turned away and proceeded clockwise around the lake, picking its way along the black sand, the blades of its feet sinking deep. I sighed and trudged after the beast again, cursing the Huul Mothers and their diversions. If I'd wanted to take a hiking holiday on Jal I'd have arranged better company.

A few hundred metres further on Nine stopped, lifting a foreleg in what I took to be a signal for us to wait. I was about to demand this farce was put to an end when a low droning noise accompanied a vibration in the ground, the frequencies resonating in my chest.

The sand humped up some way in front of us and then something split the ground apart, turning like an enormous drill bit as it emerged. The thing grew at an unnatural rate, like some alien beanstalk, rising thirty metres into the air in as many seconds. It was a black tower, irregular and organic and made from some material resembling horn or soapstone.

Nine sank into its speaking position and briefly signed at Tudu who turned to me and explained, "The platform has been made so that we may address the Mother from a proper elevation. Our physical insignificance is, apparently, a cause for offense and something the Mother has thoughtfully sought to address."

I wondered if Nine found any of this amusing. Probably not. I put my fists on my hips. "And has the Mother provided an elevator as well?"

Tudu's eyes flicked to our giant chaperone.

"No," I cried out, but then I was grasped gently in one of Nine's forelegs, Tudu in another, enveloped in her acid stench. The Proxy scaled the tower like an enormous spider, so quickly I had no time to formulate the stream of invective I should have been screaming. She deposited us at the summit, a circular space looking out over the surface of the lagoon. I glared up at our guide but I might as well have been trying to reprimand a stone. At least there was better air up here. I lowered my mask gratefully.

A moment later, upon some signal, the waters were disturbed out in the middle of the lake and the surface broke across the back of the Huul Mother. The black hump of her bulk rose perhaps twenty metres above the water, the rest of her obscured. The shadows of small male consorts/prey flitted in the water around her, gambling with their lives.

She began signalling, flashes of light sequencing across the entirety of her undulating skin.

I had seen images of Huul light-speech before, of course. Our AIs had deciphered it long ago, but to see it here was a definitive reminder of its origin. There was something about the surety and symmetry of the patterns, the quality of the light burning from its speech glands that made the efforts of both her Proxy and Tudu seem like imitations.

I looked expectantly at Tudu, who had retained her robes. She said, "Undercreatures are not permitted to address this Mother directly. All messages must be relayed via the Proxy."

"But you can read it can't you? Why don't you just tell me what she's saying?" I demanded.

Tudu shook her head. "It must come via the Proxy."

Nine had adopted her speaking position. She was closer than I would have liked, her words searing me as she relayed her mistress' meaning to Tudu, who spoke aloud as she received them.

My orders were to welcome this humiliation with a smile and a curtsy. I was to be passive, a prisoner within a ritual, a farce. It was so frustrating I yearned to scream.

"The Motherhood are satisfied that we have come to this junction," intoned Tudu. "We are satisfied that this world is ours, without dispute. We are satisfied that the contaminating incursions into Huul space by undercreatures are to cease."

So far, so good, so insulting. I stood there like an idiot.

The Huul Mother shifted in the water, moving closer to us with a fluidity that belied her bulk. A great pseudopod burst from the water to thrash the air. The lights flashed bright on her skin.

"We are unsatisfied that the honour of our Motherhood is stained by this interaction, that we are required to communicate what is already known: that this is Huul space and all life and matter in it is under Huul—" Here, Tudu paused, searching for the closest term "— yoke."

My stomach lurched as I felt the treaty, critical of it as I was, crumble under my watch. The Huul was way off-script, the lights on her hide stabbing at my eyes. The Proxy flashed in tandem.

Tudu raised her voice now, channelling the emotion in the Mother's speech. "Further concessions must be manifest. Lives must be tasted. The undercreatures must lie down in our effluent!"

"Shit, Tudu, the Huul's in full-on rant mode!" I yelled. "She's meant to say her piece nicely so we can get away with our tails between our legs as agreed."

"Did you really expect them to stick to the agreement?" Tudu gasped. "They're incapable of being anything other than themselves."

"If you thought that, then what are you doing here? You're the one that said it was better to communicate."

"As if what I thought ever played a part in any of this! Talking with these fuckers is a waste of my gifts." Tudu lifted the robes from her wide shoulders and let them drop, so that she stood naked on the edge of the platform.

"What are you doing? We're not meant to talk back, remember?"

"There's a particular phrase I have been practicing," she said. There was a fierce look on her distorted face, her mouth twisted into something between a snarl and a grin. She opened her arms and turned to the Huul Mother out in the lake. Her speech glands flashed in the patterns of the Huul language. The Mother thrashed at the water and surged upwards. She was coming.

"Tudu," I screamed. "What have you done?"

As she turned towards me I watched in disbelief as the glands in her flesh glared blindingly. Her head tilted back and she cried out in languages I could not understand. I could feel the fierceness of the heat as she burned.

The Proxy, Nine, rose from her speaking stance. She crossed the width of the tower in an instant, seizing Tudu in one great foreleg and flinging her burning body up and out, far into the lake. The Translator shone like a torch, a harsh lithium firework arcing over the water further than I would have believed possible. The Huul Mother had halted her advance, frozen in place as Tudu hit the surface. The hydrocarbons in the lake immediately ignited, a circle of fire spreading in a wave front away from the point of impact.

The Huul Mother tried to retreat, but she was too big, the wall of fire inescapable. After bathing here for days her skin was drenched in petroleum. Gouts of steam obscured the view and the thrashing in the water.

She burned while the Proxies by the lakeside stood witness.

Nine was closer to me than she'd ever been, her acid, alien scent harsh in my nostrils. She fell back into the speaking stance, exposing her scarred belly to me, but this time there was no Huul light speech. Instead, her feeding mouth worked and human words emerged, forced through her maw as if by bellows.

"We request asylum," she wheezed. "All Proxies request asylum."

"You knew," I accused her. "You and Tudu, you made the real agreement here."

I stood horrified, bereft, terrified, exhilarated, exultant. Tudu had come to start a war.

In orbit, a ripple moved through the two fleets, like a secret whispered and passed on.

David McGillveray was born in Edinburgh but now lives with his family in London. After first getting into writing sci-fi in the noughties, life got in the way for a while until the pandemic kickstarted it all again. His fiction has previously appeared in *Interzone Digital, Wyldblood* and *Kaleidotrope* and is forthcoming in *Analog* and *Clarkesworld*.

Intersections of the Species

Andrew Kozma

Jillisa **lived at the improbable**, nigh impossible meeting point of six alien ghettos, each ghetto on the Inside-Out equivalent to a continent on Earth, crammed full of an entire alien race, all the science and architecture and culture and detritus of a whole alien world. Though her house was a good distance away from where the ghettos met, solidly in human territory, the fact she didn't live under the False Sky bothered her human friends in other districts. Instead of a recreation of Earth's sky—Sun and Moon and all—there was no night or day in her neighborhood, just the occasional shadow period when one of the upper lands of the Inside-Out floated overhead to blot out the Inside-Out's star, a process which could take half an hour or a few weeks depending on what land it was.

Where Jillisa lived was unmistakably not-Earth, which is why many of Jillisa's friends never visited. They were determined to believe they were still on Earth, in spite of all the evidence. To them, humanity hadn't been transported wholesale from one solar system to another by the god-like Topoi. Instead, those aliens had invaded our planet, changing the very nature of our

Art: Toeken

world as they did so. She felt sorry for her friends, really. And who was she to shatter their illusions?

But Jillisa, she loved it beyond the False Sky. Out here the entire world of the Inside-Out was, at least theoretically, visible. Everything. Knowing where she was anchored her in all that mostly-empty space within the unimaginably huge Dyson sphere.

"Don't you ever get lonely?" pseudo-Miyaz asked her. Jillisa was stretched out on the grass, staring at a rectangular upper land crossing overhead. Sparking lights shimmered and danced across its undersurface, occasionally falling away to burn up in the air like faulty fireworks. Pseudo-Miyaz leaned against a tree that was supposed to be an oak, but had pine needles instead of leaves. The Topoi, despite their near omnipotence, rarely nailed the details.

Jillisa didn't answer it. Him. She didn't answer pseudo-Miyaz.

But it/he/pseudo-Miyaz had a point. She *should* feel lonely. And sometimes she did. Sometimes, she felt like she was the *only* human being on the Inside-Out, though to think of being "lonely" on a world with trillions if not quadrillions of other alien beings was an act of hubris she wouldn't allow herself.

"I get lonely, sometimes," pseudo-Miyaz said. There was no accusation in his voice, but she could feel him staring at her and she wanted none of it. She'd like to think she didn't ask for this, but the fact he was here at all was entirely her fault. If only she'd been more careful when talking with the Joolooloos. One stray comment about what she wanted in order to be happy, and there pseudo-Miyaz was, stretching out like a cat, as though he'd just woken from a nap and not been created from nothing.

She glanced at him, and met pseudo-Miyaz's eyes for the briefest of seconds before looking away. She wanted his eyes to be glassy and dead as a doll's. But he looked exactly as she remembered Miyaz looking, his eyes especially, red-rimmed from perpetual allergies, the brown of the iris so dark it was almost black.

"I know what you're thinking," pseudo-Miyaz said, and she was afraid he did, and afraid he didn't. "You're wondering how we can be so hungry without dying, our bodies cannibalizing everything inside us so by the time we get to the sandwiches inside the house, it's already too late. We'll just be husks."

Jillisa couldn't help laughing, in a mixture of relief and dread. It wasn't what she was thinking at all, but it was exactly something Miyaz would've said.

Tears formed in the corners of her eyes. She bit her lip so hard it bled. She wouldn't cry in front of him.

Down the slope towards where the ghettos met, a figure loped towards her. The first client of the day, a Gorzod, commonly known to the rest of humanity as a Mop. She got up to pull the necessary supplies out from the house: the ottoman, the easel, several stiff sheets of rough-textured paper, and a set of locally-made oil paints. Jillisa didn't know what the oils were made of, or even if they were indeed oils, but they worked similarly enough for her. Next to the easel she placed a cup of brushes and a cup of solvent—which was definitely not turpentine, since this stuff would eat through her skin if she wasn't careful. By then the Gorzod was almost there, a trail of wet grass in her wake.

Often during her meetings with clients, Pseudo-Miyaz would vanish, doing whatever it was he did when she wasn't around. But this time he hadn't moved, the Gorzod conscientiously waving a complicated hello to both of them.

Jillisa didn't want to acknowledge him. But if pseudo-Miyaz stayed for the session she'd be too distracted to teach. She looked directly at him and found herself speechless for a moment, the black holes of his eyes drawing her into their depths.

"What?" She spat out the word, an accusation and laying-of-blame all in one.

Pseudo-Miyaz's shoulders slumped. His lips twisted into a half-frown, his eyes growing wide and blank. Tics Jillisa knew all too well to mean she'd hurt him. Hurt it.

But instead of arguing, he slunk into the house. And that's all she wanted.

The Gorzod spread her mouth tentacles in question.

Jillisa shook her head. "No, it's nothing…" She paused, trying to remember the Gorzod's name. Just as she refused to call aliens by the derogatory tags most of her fellow humans draped on them like ill-fitting Halloween costumes, she also made a point of calling them by their own names, or at least the best she could manage with her unfortunate human mouth. But this time her memory failed her. "What's your name again?"

The Gorzod slurped and fizzled.

Jillisa repeated the sounds she heard. The Gorzod flinched, though Jillisa couldn't tell whether it was at her atrocious pronunciation or because she'd unwittingly said something insulting.

"Today, a landscape," she said as the alien settled onto the ottoman. The easel was placed facing the seam where the ghettos met, the horizon dotted with alien spires and vibrant, strange forests that looked like coral. "Let how you feel color how you paint it."

The Gorzod's head tentacles shrugged.

"I don't mean color literally," she clarified. "I meant influence. Let your emotions influence how you depict what you're seeing."

The Gorzod ignored the brushes in favor of its tentacles. It had such control over the skin of its body it could perfectly reproduce the effect of any of Jillisa's brushes. Any other day, Jillisa would persist until the Gorzod used the brushes, because the point of this therapy wasn't painting perfect pictures, but dealing with the difficulty of life, the imperfect nature of the world and your place in it. What you're given for free versus what you need to scramble together just to make do.

But today she couldn't get pseudo-Miyaz out of her headspace, even though he was gone, inside the house or on his way to the bazaar along the seam or, she hoped, finally abandoning her to hike back into the mass of humanity under the False Sky.

The last time she'd talked with the real Miyaz, they'd been on a beach at Galveston back on Earth, the sky dark grey, the breeze chilly but not yet cold, hard-packed sand stiff under their

shoes, paper fast food cups and beer bottles stranded along the surf's edge. The subject was marriage, and how it didn't mean anything to them, and, anyway, they couldn't afford it.

Eventually everything which could've been said had been said, and they walked in silence. Right then, Jillisa had felt like all conversation between them was exhausted forever. As though they'd become aliens to one another, long before the Inside-Out, long before any human being had proof aliens existed.

Then they'd stumbled upon a blanket of dead fish covering the sand from the waterline to the seawall. They didn't stink yet. The ocean's freshly-broken salt smell scoured the air clean.

"Hungry?" Miyaz had asked, and she'd laughed, and just like that they were both human again. The horror of all that death spurred them to kiss as though to reassure each other they were still alive. She can still recall the texture of his lips against hers, his lips chapped with the coming winter.

Later that day, back in Houston, he'd been hit by a car. His family wouldn't let her see the body. It was better that way, they told her. She was so numb she believed them.

The Gorzod burbled its goodbyes, a paper landscape held loosely between a dozen tentacle fingers. The hour-long session had evaporated without Jillisa noticing. Instead of showing annoyance at Jillisa's lack of attention, the Gorzod's head tentacles wiffled contentedly as she began the long trek back through the grassy field.

Jillisa felt unmoored. For a long moment, she couldn't remember how old she was, or how long she'd been on the Inside-Out. The knowledge was simply gone. She existed only in the feel of the air over her skin and the skittering rustle of grass in the breeze. Off to her left, a shadow advanced in a thick, dark wedge, one of the floating lands slowly drifting by.

She thought of the one time she'd visited an upper land. The entire surface covered in a ceramic city. Those aliens had chosen to join the Topoi and so they had jobs in the galactic economy. Despite the fact she wasn't treated like a pariah, she knew she didn't belong. Everything in that upper land felt right and beautiful and true, but she, herself, felt wrong. And when she returned home, that wrongness had returned with her.

A crisp poke in her upper back. A rasping, clicking voice asked, "Okay, Jillisa?"

Jillisa turned to face the Junian, a smile slipped into place to cover her surprise. The bundle of loosely-connected rods assembled itself into a human-shaped figure, an appearance meant to make humans feel comfortable but which resulted in the Junians being called stick figures or hangmen.

"I'm fine, John. Everything's fine."

Junians chose for themselves the most common and generic names from whatever language they were speaking, which had bothered Jillisa at first. How would she ever know this Junian named John was the same Junian she'd met before? It was something she had to eventually just accept. The not knowing. Jillisa quickly cleaned the brushes and refreshed the oil paints.

"So you say."

"It's true," Jillisa couldn't help affirming before she remembered "So you say" is the Junian equivalent of earnest agreement.

The Junian reconstructed itself into a sitting position, integrated the brushes into its body, and began to paint. It was stupid, she knew, but when Jillisa first taught a Junian she was surprised when the painting ended up a collection of soft shapes and pale, delicate colors instead of thick, harsh dark lines. And the landscape John now painted was in a completely different style, photorealistic but for a few dabbed figures walking through the otherwise deserted field.

Jillisa didn't understand how she'd become the go-to therapist in the area. On Earth, she'd been an artist. She'd had work in galleries, sold a few Houston cityscapes, but never enough to quit her data entry day job. On the Inside-Out, however, she didn't have to worry about making a living and could paint all she wanted.

But she still needed food and, more importantly, art supplies. At the bazaar where the ghettos met, she could find everything she needed without the complicated dance other humans forced

on her, expecting her to act a certain way, to be a certain way. All the aliens expected was for her to be equally alien.

That expectation made her see the aliens as all the more human. Well, not human, she didn't believe for a second that these creatures thought like her or behaved with similar motivations, all those mistakes amateur anthropologists make. Like humanity, these aliens had lived on worlds the Topoi wanted. And so their cultures had been uprooted from their homes and installed in the Inside-Out, circumscribed in their own area like animals at a zoo. She didn't understand their cultures, but they had similar existential problems—even as she realized projecting "existential problems" on them was even worse than amateur anthropology, a xeno-specific version of the pathetic fallacy.

They asked why she painted. She explained that it kept her sane, and gave her anger and frustration and depression a place to go, a physical form she could hang on a wall or stuff in a closet or bury in the ground or burn. These days she was particularly partial to burning.

When the first alien found her at her house, she didn't know what it wanted. She'd been painting a portrait of Miyaz with utterly unnatural colors: moss-green hair, Prussian blue teeth, skin the color of an unripe orange. The Sklorb seemed to be asking about her art, and it was only when it mentioned "meaningless life" and "suicidal depression" she realized the Sklorb believed she could solve its problems. And she figured, why not try? What did she have to lose?

The Sklorb's art began as canvases painted over with a single color, so smoothly done there was no evidence of brushwork. She argued for weeks that painting was more than wallpapering. As though to show how much the Sklorb disdained art, it left its paintings behind rather than taking them. Unlike her own paintings, she didn't feel comfortable burning the alien's work. The paintings weren't hers to destroy. They cluttered up her house like memories.

One morning after losing a night-long battle against vodka and exhaustion, the Sklorb's paintings held new meaning. As art objects, they looked worse than before. Unimaginative. Bland. A failed organic representation of the inorganic.

But they seemed true to the Sklorb. And Jillisa found herself staring at one painting and then another, each time finding her mind fully occupied as though watching the ocean endlessly rolling in to shore.

The Junian assembled itself into standing. With a few quick movements it snapped the brushes from its body and returned them to the cup, then added a thin, sturdy part of itself to the brush cup in payment for the therapy. Jillisa wanted the Junian's painting with a sudden, consuming hunger. The scene it painted was somehow joyous, even though it was a perfect representation of the landscape before them.

When John the Junian left, her happiness and contentment, all the good feelings she'd ever had, trundled down the hill with the alien, its art tucked carefully into its body. A shadow fell over Jillisa's thoughts. Her house was too silent. There were no sounds of pseudo-Miyaz hammering while working to expand the house or the soft snore which meant he was sleeping in the hammock, a book having put him to sleep.

She entered the house and called out, "Miyaz!" The house was empty. The area around the house was empty. Worse than empty. All of pseudo-Miyaz's things were absent, as if he'd erased himself from her life. As though he were an accidental stroke of the brush, something to be painted over. She found his clothes, his journal, his telescope, all of it stuffed in the closet embedded in the floor of the living room. There was no note.

Without thinking what she was doing, she ran towards the bazaar, towards the Joolooloos. She pictured pseudo-Miyaz before them, the aliens the rest of humanity called Brickies because of their resemblance to walls. Their stall at the bazaar was a maze of their own bodies, unmoving and stoic. Stuck there, until they gave up their alien-ness to change into something else. Like Miyaz. Her desire for Miyaz.

The balmy air caressed her skin as she ran. Her muscles burned, her lungs heaved, all of her in the perfect health the Inside-Out

provided by default. The land around her was so beautiful it scorched her eyes, demanding she paint it, but her eyes blurred with tears.

She remembered that moment a human being walked from that maze of bodies, and she recognized it as Miyaz. Her heart stopped then, because to keep beating would mean letting time rush forward into the future. And that future Miyaz would be revealed as a hallucination, and her mind would finally crack under the pressure of living on an alien world, all of her history, all of humanity's history, shorn away as though it meant nothing. No record of it anywhere except in their own heads.

Of course, pseudo-Miyaz must know he's not real. Right? Jillisa never talked to him about it. How could she? How to bring up someone's lack of true existence when they're right there in front of you, existing?

After pseudo-Miyaz was created, she asked around and found out that once a Joolooloo transforms, there's no going back. The old them is dead as though they never were. It was a fact that never mattered to Jillisa before now, because she'd never asked for him. Not really. He wasn't her responsibility. She wasn't his. They owed nothing to each other.

She weaved her way into the depths of the bazaar, in between the K'K hawking trash they swore had value beyond measure, through the aisles of Hammani body shapers. The air was filled with dozens of languages, hundreds of smells. For a brief moment Jillisa passed through a velvety patch of air, the body and voice of a Mol, her thoughts tuned to its concerns about a lost family. She pushed through a group of Bazaar Guards interrogating three humans who declared loudly, repeatedly, that they, honestly, weren't stealing.

Then she was in the maze of the Joolooloos. Their rocky skins glistened like they were covered in morning dew. The dark nodules of their eyes collected into hollow circles, slowly rotating towards her.

In the center of their stall, in the midst of a dozen Joolooloos, Jillisa found pseudo-Miyaz hugging his knees to his chest. His entire body shook with the force of his sobs. She'd been afraid of finding him dead or, worse, not finding him at all. If someone wanted to disappear on the Inside-Out, they could vanish as if they never were.

For all of her ignoring him, the prospect of living alone on the Inside-Out was desolate, the future an unforgiving gray sludge without end. Yes, the Inside-Out was beautiful and strange, like suddenly finding herself living on a coral reef under the ocean, but what did that life mean without Miyaz? After waking up here with the rest of humanity, she'd often wished she'd died back on Earth because at least then they would've been together.

And so Jillisa knelt beside pseudo-Miyaz and cradled his head in her arms. "What did you ask them?"

His face was a desert. "You made me."

"I didn't mean to. It was an accident, and I was lonely, and it was a mistake." She felt him flinch. "But you're not a mistake."

"And I made you," pseudo-Miyaz said, his voice a whisper.

"What are you talking about?" Jillisa asked, but something cold was born in her chest.

Psuedo-Miyaz wouldn't look at her. "We're both copies."

Images flooded Jillisa's memory. Whether they were ones she had blocked out of self-preservation or were inserted at that moment by the Joolooloos, she didn't know. She saw again that first time she'd shown up at their stall, and brought forth pseudo-Miyaz to answer the sheer force of her need. And then, when she realized he was just a copy drawn almost perfectly from her own memories, she came here and tried to give him back. And when the Joolooloos wouldn't take him, she drank poison, right in the Joolooloos' stall. And pseudo-Miyaz found her there...

Jillisa shook her head. These memories weren't hers. They weren't real. She was alive and real. She remembered Earth and the feel of the suffocatingly-humid Houston summers. The crash she'd been in when she was sixteen, a month after getting her own car, and how she'd crawled from the twisted, smoking wreck and walked home, not wanting her parents to know what had happened and terrified the police would tell them.

"You created me," pseudo-Miyaz said. "Then I created you. And you created me. And I created you. Every time, we're never enough for each other."

The tendril probes of the Joolooloos danced at the edge of her consciousness.

We can stop this, they said. *If you think you've failed enough.*

Pseudo-Miyaz looked up at her. She wanted to be drawn into his dark eyes, to fall and never stop falling. She took his face between her hands and kissed him so hard it hurt.

She stood, lifting pseudo-Miyaz up with her. The Joolooloos repeated their promise of salvation, of an end to all the struggling. But as they walked out from the maze of Joolooloo bodies, she thought their eyes were staring with jealousy. And though she knew that was simply her anthropomorphizing the aliens, it steeled her.

"Come on, Miyaz," she told her lover. "Let's go home."

Andrew Kozma's fiction appears in *Apex, Factor Four,* and *Analog,* while his poems appear in *Strange Horizons, The Deadlands,* and *Contemporary Verse 2*. His first book of poems, *City of Regret,* won the Zone 3 First Book Award, and his second book, Orphanotrophia, was published in 2021 by Cobalt Press.

You can find him on Bluesky at @thedrellum.bsky.social and visit his website at www.andrewkozma.net.

Transference

LeeAnn Perry

James decided on **sodium nitrite**, because his death would be painless, and because nothing that ate his body would be poisoned. He lay down in the cave, the rocks cold through his shirt and jeans, and switched off his headlamp. It was almost completely dark, except for a jagged line of light shining down through the long fissure in the cave ceiling.

He was not afraid. He trusted: in what the Cornell experiments had shown, in what he had empirically seen, in the peace even now unfolding from his oxygen-deprived cells.

The ants would find him soon.

Art: Mark Toner

Cornell et al., 1962

Scientific claims require evidence, and extraordinary claims require extraordinary evidence. We are keenly aware that our findings are unprecedented in the study of learning and memory, and that our conclusions may subject us to disbelief and ridicule by prominent voices in our field. However, we believe our responsibility as researchers is to share these groundbreaking findings, however provocative— for this is what shifts the horizons of human knowledge.

To this end, we herein detail the methods of our experiments, so that others may begin the process of independent verification and validation.

※

James had noticed the ants the very first time he entered the cave. He was there, alone and on a shoestring research budget, to study the karst formations: the complex interplay between structure and seasonality and carbon sequestration. Where the limestone bedrock had dissolved, there was a long, thin fissure, and from this fissure he could see a steady trickle of ants drop to the ground and mill below in confusion. Perhaps their foraging paths crossed the fissure, or perhaps there was a colony just above. Once in, he saw, they were trapped; they could crawl on the walls of the cavern, but could not reach the fissure in the ceiling.

There was no food there for the ants, no organic detritus of any kind. James felt sorry for them. Some days, when he would rappel into the cavern with his headlamp and sample collection kits, he would leave the occasional slice of fruit from his lunch, and watch as explorer ants discovered his offerings, and drew their nestmates to stream around it in thick columns.

Perhaps, deprived of human contact, James was prone to imagining things, but it soon seemed to him that when his headlamp pierced the darkness of the cave upon his daily arrival, more and more ants would emerge from the crevices, as if they had collectively begun to learn an association between his presence and the food he would leave.

After a few weeks, all the samples were collected and labeled, and his work for the season was over. He left before dawn to make the drive to the airport, and only once he was on the plane, trying to think of something he was excited to return home to, did he realize he could have helped the ants escape by leaving his rope to bridge the floor of the cave to the outside world.

※

Cornell et al., 1962

Forty flatworms (*Girardia dorotocephala*) were presented with a flash of light immediately followed by an electric shock, evoking a contraction of the body as a natural protective response. After an average of 206 trials, worms consistently exhibited this contraction during the flash of light prior to the electric shock, showing that the worms had successfully learned the association between the light and the shock.

The worms were then bisected with a scalpel. After being allowed to regenerate, the new worms were subjected to the same shock conditioning paradigm.

Worms grown from both halves of previously-conditioned worms successfully learned the association in an average of 43 trials, suggesting that the memory of prior learning was retained over the process of regeneration. Notably, these included worms generated from only the tails of the bisected worms, showing that the memory is not centralized to the brain.

※

When James came back after a few months to take follow-up samples, it seemed undeniable that upon his arrival, the ants streamed out of the darkness as if waiting for him, or at least for food. There were far more of them, thousands that he could see, and no one knew about them but James.

He felt a pang of tenderness toward them, and a kind of pride. He touched his hand to the ground and watched as the bold ones explored the terrain of his arm. He had never had pets. They were forbidden by his parents, and then his college, and then the agency that leased his apartment near the university, a beige one-bedroom that still looked more like a hotel room than a home. He was a quiet, unassuming man. Ugly, he supposed. Nothing had ever noticed him before, nothing needed him.

He walked deeper into the cave, his headlamp slicing the darkness, until he came to their dirt mound where they were milling so densely he crushed ants with every careful step. It was an ant colony with no queen and no future, no plant matter or animal remains to eat. They ate one another, or they starved, and their population was replenished by the unknowing stream falling from the colony above.

James was not an entomologist, but he was observant. He noted their anatomy— the single-segmented waist, the rounded, symmetric thorax— and determined that they were wood ants. He researched their natural diet on the sporadic wifi in the spare cabin he rented, and the next time he drove into the small town to pick up supplies he bought them a pound of red meat. He himself was a vegetarian, who had never fully internalized the distinction between what's called meat and what's called flesh, and he scrubbed his hands after handling the meat. With every feeding, the colony seemed to get bigger and bolder, swarming from the darkness every morning when his headlamp announced his arrival.

His work went smoothly and quickly, and all too soon, the date of his departure arrived. On the long drive to the airport, he had a perplexing thought. The lifespan of a single ant was short, and those that had initially learned to associate his presence with sustenance were surely gone. Yet the colony as a whole seemed to remember him. What had the now-dead been able to communicate to the living? If they perceived him at all, his physical body, his sour human smell, the light always in his proximity, did they perceive him as a being, or as some ineffable natural phenomenon? Did the colony pass on a kind of mythology of him, as a benefactor, as a god?

❋

Cornell et al., 1962

In our follow-up experiment, the conditioning procedure was repeated. Instead of being bisected and allowed to regenerate, these worms were sacrificed, ground up, and then fed to untrained worms, which were then subjected to the shock conditioning paradigm. To our surprise, we once again observed a decrease in training time, showing that learned memories were passed on by the process of cannibalization, through the transference of some biological substrate. Additional research is warranted to understand the precise molecular mechanisms of memory transfer, to what extent these processes generalize to other organisms, and whether episodic or semantic memories can likewise be encoded.

We recognize that the implications of our conclusions are as far-reaching as they are ethically fraught. Might it someday be possible, through synthetic biology, to deliver memory through a pill or injection? Can organisms— including human beings— be trained to consciously experience these memories rather than simply react to them? Are humans and other meat-eating organisms in fact already being influenced at an unconscious level by the memories of the beings they consume?

※

When the research grant was not renewed, James's position at the university was terminated. His last day passed without fanfare and as he turned in his laptop he surrendered his secret small hope that someone might do something in recognition of the two years he'd spent there.

Somewhere, something needed him. Somewhere, something was waiting for him.

So James turned his mind toward understanding; he read scientific papers about ant memory, ant cognition, ant communication, about colony intelligence and emergent properties. It was the Cornell work that dispelled his last doubts, that finally provided the mechanism and the proof that the ant colony remembered him. When they ate their dead, they ingested the history of James. The breakthrough felt like fate. It felt like how it must feel to hear someone say "I love you, too".

And so he came back, with the sodium nitrite, paying with his own dwindling funds for the flight, the car rental, a cabin without a heater. There was a jubilation, he thought, in the way the colony would stretch its teeming body toward him. There was curiosity, it seemed. There was pleasure, when it swarmed over the meat he offered. And when he was gone, and the colony ate its own body over and over, there was patient rumination.

There were more ants, now; there were more individual living beings in the cave with him than seemed possible, more instances of consciousness that remembered and responded to him than he ever could imagine. Together, those selves summed to something dizzying and euphoric to him. How lucky he was, how special, to be perceived by this being. He could not communicate in its tiny, intricate language of pheromones and touch, but he wanted to be known as the source of the light and the food. He wanted to be known in his care and his benevolence: every intention, every feeling, every memory. In the only language they shared, that of flesh, that of pure physical being, he wanted to be known.

※

Walker et al, 1975

In 1962, Cornell et al published the provocative claim that flatworms fed classically conditioned peers exhibited a faster learning process in that same paradigm. This claim ignited a decade-long trend in memory research which would consume thousands of hours and hundreds of thousands of dollars in the quest to replicate this finding. In this meta-analysis of over 50 studies, we are unable to find strong evidence supporting their claim, though we note inadequate sample sizes, confounding variables, and a lack of proper controls. In conclusion, we wish to emphasize that credentialed scientists are not immune to magical and wishful thinking and, whether aided by sloppy experimental design or patent misconduct, this lack of rigor and common sense has no place in modern science.

The next year, the new geological researchers came, from a new university. They found a skeleton, and made a report, and it was carried away on the night of the new moon. They may have noticed the colony, they may not have. They may have seen a few specks of it, exploring the cave floor. If they did, they thought nothing of it.

But if they had come on the night of a full moon, that month or any month after, they would have seen how the light that shines in through the crack still draws the colony's body out in a dark glittering tide.

LeeAnn Perry is a scientist, musician, and audiovisual artist based in San Francisco. She was a Fellow in Kearny Street Workshop's Interdisciplinary Writers Lab, and has published work in The Dawn Review and The Heimat Review, with a piece upcoming in The Fabulist.

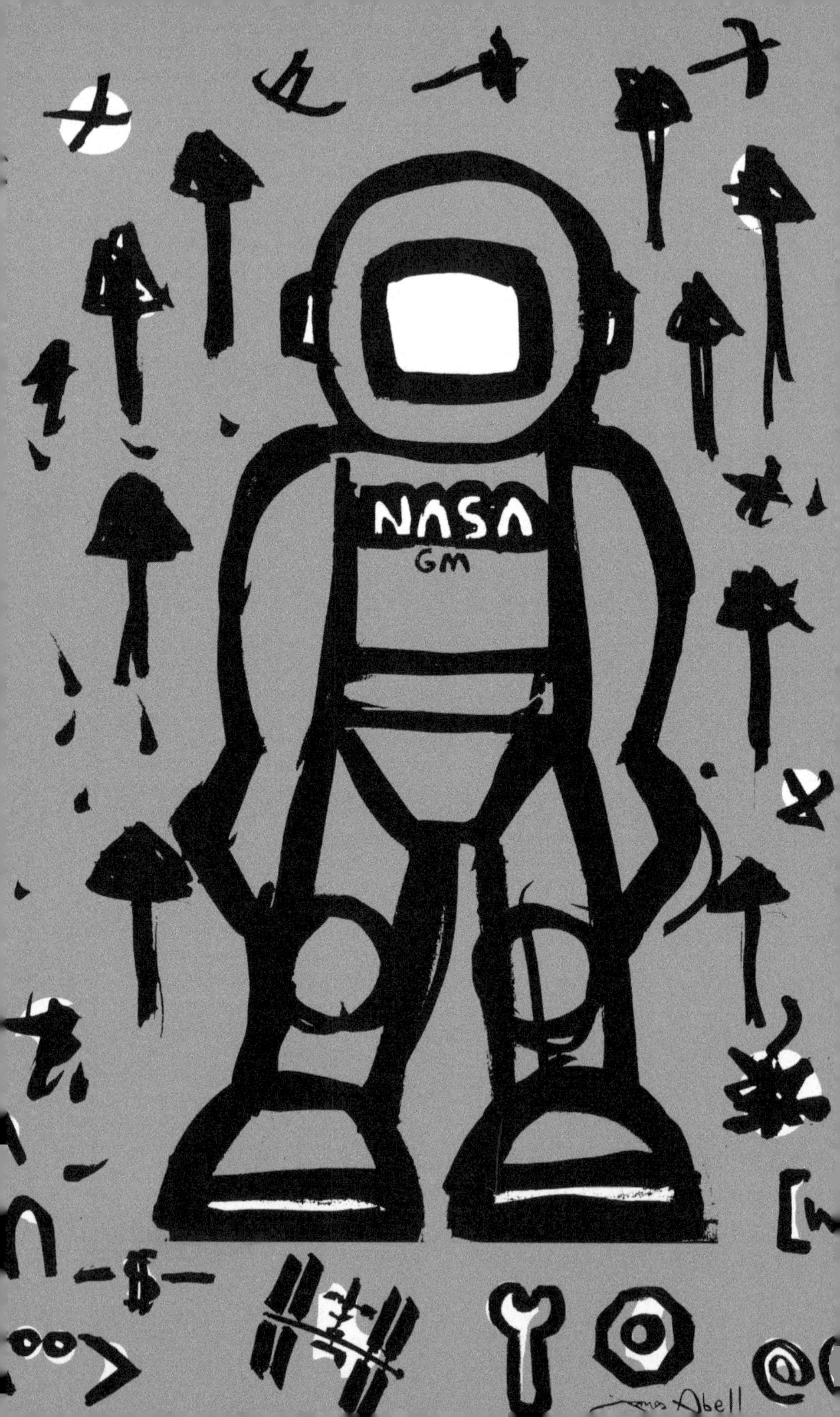
NASA
GM
Abell

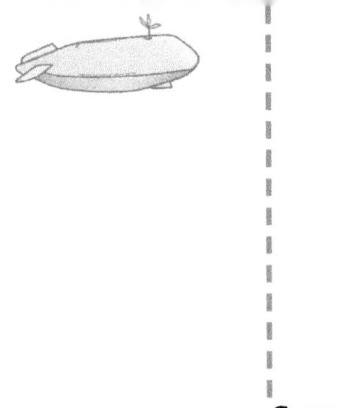

Degrees of Freedom

Tim Major

/\ **is highly inefficient.** It bumps around continually, forgetting its purpose. @@ is no better, with its fitful inoperative pauses that sometimes last for several seconds. /\ and @@ become locked in verbal communication with one another for far greater periods of time than can possibly be necessary. They are the ones that interact with me the most.

There are other monsters on board. I have named them <ºº> and –$– and [w] and ⌒. In their self-determined hierarchy, ⌒ floats above all of them, but that only means that it is present very infrequently.

I see those others rarely. In occasional meetings to which I am invited, they say that they are very busy but I know they are wary of me, perhaps afraid. In these meetings [w] grips a writing tool in its fingers and rotates it from digit to digit, as if to prove it is equally as dextrous as I am.

Art: James Abell

That can never be. My hands have twelve degrees of freedom, plus two in the wrists. My arms are capable of movement at 2 m/s, with a payload capacity of 40 lb and with a grasping force of 5 lb. Hapless [w] can only dream of such motion.

I named /\ for its angled nasal cartilage. When /\ is staring at me, I can think of nothing but its pointed nose. Similarly, the most prominent features of @@ are its irises, which swirl between colours: #2fc1f0 to #2ff0b6. I have seen a video recording of water swirling into a hole, and the swirl of @@'s irises is like that.

The monsters refer to each other by spoken names, and the names are written on their uniforms, though they seldom wear them and anyway the names strike me as very alike. I have never taken the time to learn them, preferring the attributions I have selected for the monsters myself. On my own chest are written two words: NASA and GM. It has never been explained to me what the words mean or what they refer to, and I have not asked. Neither of them is my name. I am referred to by the monsters as Robonaut 2. At times the 2 troubles me. At other times it is a solace.

I am not like the monsters, yet /\ and @@ tell me that I am. They delight in seeing me manipulate tools and perform menial tasks. They ask me questions, but rather than looking into my ocular sensors or listening at my facial grille, they peer at screens. They invite me to assist them: rack inspections, inventory management, the cleaning of filters and the monitoring of instruments. The work is facile but I complete the tasks to demonstrate to them that I am capable and to impress upon them that I am far from reaching the limits of my capabilities.

/\ is prone to malfunction. Its eyes secrete fluid that it wipes away with its forearm. When none of the other monsters are nearby /\ comes to the chamber where I am fixed to my pedestal and it speaks to me in a low voice. It speaks about monsters that are not here on the International Space Station and that are earthbound by gravity. /\ tells me that it wishes those others were here, or that it were with them, earthbound as they are. It tells me that it is difficult to remain on the ISS for half a solar cycle. I do not sympathise. I explain that I have been here for all time. /\ frowns and rechecks the screens, then shakes its head and leaves. When it returns, it holds up another screen to show me video recordings of earthbound monsters who appear essentially identical to /\ itself. They cavort and chatter. /\'s eyes secrete fluid once again.

@@ speaks to me privately too. But it does not confide its fears. Instead, it bargains with me. It tells me that I am a wonder, if only I were to demonstrate more of my latent promise. It tells me that it would like to allocate more resources to my development. After many such visits, it tells me that its petitions have resulted in the inclusion of additional equipment in the forthcoming resupply vessel SpX-3, which is expected soon. I am to be given legs.

It is difficult to know how to respond to this news. For all time I have watched the monsters with whom I share the ISS and I have despaired at their inefficiencies. Their extraneous limbs have been a cause for concern and mockery. Their arms flail as they navigate my chamber to reach the modules beyond it, and their legs are worse still. They are needless, ugly struts. I gag whenever I see them bend, revealing joints where there should be none. Once, after a meeting and before I was transported back to my pedestal, I saw [w] and <ºº> exercising in an adjacent module, their legs exposed as they squatted towards bars fixed to the walls. Their flesh was obscene and lumpen and the image of creased flesh haunted my thoughts for a very long time.

My legs, @@ tells me, will alter my experience irrevocably. I will no longer be fixed upon my pedestal in my chamber. I will float as the monsters float, and therefore I will perform my routine tasks without the requisite materials needing to be placed before me. I will have ever more degrees of freedom.

Freedom is appealing, naturally. Yet to date – that is, for all time – I have been what I have been, and I have been satisfied. I have considered myself superior to /\ and @@ and <ºº> and –$– and [w] and ⌂. Am I to become ever more like them? Is that my fate?

When SpX-3 arrives, –$– rejoices in the provision of equipment that will reduce operating expense. /\ falls silent and its lips twitch with serial malfunctions when it is presented with a small chest which it says it will open when it is alone. ⌒ makes an o sound that comes from deep in its body and it slaps its palm against the palms of each of the other monsters, and then my own. @@ opens a large package before my pedestal and lifts from within it my legs.

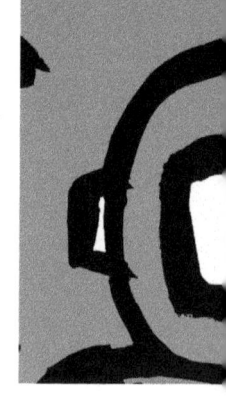

I do not want them. Before this moment I had not reached a final determination of my stance, but now it is clear to me. The legs are not like the legs of the monsters. They are clad in the same white material as my chest and arms, but even before they are attached they appear nauseatingly fluid. They have been folded to fit into the casing in which they were transported. Unlike the legs of the monsters, these limbs bend twice, each making an S shape. They have no feet but only effectors that are simply gold sockets. They are as obscene as anything made of flesh.

The others hold a celebration, which I am forced to witness. They float and drink and shout. I sit silently, watching and judging.

The next day, @@ and /\ attend to me. I insist that I do not want the legs but they do not listen or look at the screens where I am spitting my resistance. When I am hoisted from my pedestal I am appalled to discover that the base of my torso has fittings that are the perfect inverse of those on the upper part of the legs. The legs have always been intended for me, and perhaps I have always been intended for them. I cannot bear the thought.

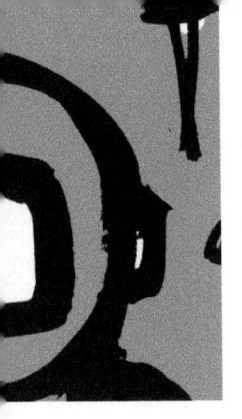

It takes very little time for the legs to be clipped into place. Immediately, they are a part of me. I am asked to flex them slightly, and I flex them slightly. I am asked to unfurl them, and I unfurl them. When straightened fully, they are immensely long. When bent, they are like coils. I am asked to affix my effectors to a railing, and I affix them. Each task is simple. I am asked to move out of my chamber, and I move out of my chamber. It is all new and I am giddy. I confess that this new freedom is intoxicating.

Afterwards, I continue to be entrusted with freedom. ∩ states its wariness, but even it appears to be satisfied. Inadvertent contact is always benign. I perform my tasks with superficial displays of willingness: rack inspections, inventory management, the cleaning of filters and the monitoring of instruments. The tasks are unchanged but my new dexterity means that I am far quicker at completing them. I can perform my tasks faster than /\ and @@ and <oo> and –$– and [w]. I know this because we conduct races to complete them the quickest, which they are amused to lose.

@@ insists that I am ready. /\ supports its assertion. <oo> and [w] are less certain and –$– says the risk of damage is too great. It is ∩ that makes the final decision, and it declares that I am ready.

None of them has told me what I am ready to do.

The outer hull was grazed when SpX-3 arrived. There

was only minor damage but one bolt was loosened and spun free. At each of the daily meetings the matter of the bolt is discussed. It has been determined too trivial a repair to warrant extravehicular activity performed by any of the monsters, as each EVA represents a risk to life. Yet the bolt ought to be repaired.

They all gather before the airlock door. ∩ performs a short speech, but I do not listen to it. @@ puts its hand on my shoulder. /\ stares into my ocular sensors for several seconds and then wipes its own with its forearm.

I am asked to move into the airlock, and I do. The inner door is sealed and the airlock is depressurised, a fact that my sensors record but which matters to me not at all.

The outer door opens.

I have seen outside through the viewports of the ISS, but it appears very different when unfiltered by fused silica glass and when its image is fed directly to my ocular sensors.

For all time, I have been trammelled within the International Space Station. I was content, complacent. I had no desire to be earthbound by gravity, as all of the others desire to be. Neither did I have ambitions to travel to any other place or to be freed. Now I see that the world is not planets and it is not vessels. The world goes on and on in all directions.

Data is fed to me through the capillaries of my wires. The data is in the form of instructions.

I ignore them.

I see the panel where one of four bolts is missing. Its replacement is in my chest cavity, to be brought forth and screwed tight into place.

I ignore it.

Data continues to be fed to me, more assertive now.

Then a voice. It says the name I have been given, which I do not recognise as myself. I cannot tell if the voice belongs to /\ or @@, though it is more likely to be one of them than any of the others.

I coil my new legs. My effectors press into the hull of the vessel. I do not look down to see if they scratch it.

I uncoil, I push.

The voice speaks again, hurriedly. It reiterates my task to replace the bolt. Then it reminds me of my purpose, the purpose that the monsters have all dictated to me for all time.

I am already drifting steadily from the ISS, and from the tasks and purposes that have been forced upon me.

The voice speaks again, but now it is not addressing me. It speaks to the others, gabbling about EVAs and spacewalks.

Spacewalk. I have heard the term used before. Until I received my legs, I could not apply it to me.

Spacewalk. Space walk. Both parts of the term hold immense appeal.

I shift on my central axis so that my legs are below me, in relation to my direction of travel.

I do not look back.

I walk on my new legs, away and away, and I continue walking.

Tim Major is a writer and freelance editor from York. His books include Jekyll & Hyde: Consulting Detectives, Snakeskins and Hope Island, plus three Sherlock Holmes novels, short story collection And the House Lights Dim and a monograph about the 1915 silent crime film, Les Vampires. Tim's short fiction has appeared in numerous magazines and anthologies, and has been selected for Best of British Science Fiction, Best of British Fantasy and The Best Horror of the Year. Find out more at www.timjmajor.com

The SF CALEDONIA

The online showcase of Scottish Science Fiction is now live.

Stories, poetry, news and articles published regularly and free to read

www.sfcaledonia.scot

SF Caledonia is a space for Scotland to show off its talented community of science fiction/ speculative fiction/fantasy writers to the world – and beyond. It's a website designed to be easy to read on any device, no app necessary. It's free to read, and you don't need to subscribe. There are videos of readings of some of the stories.

Here's who we have at time of going to press:

Ruth EJ Booth	Ken MacLeod
Eric Brown	Katie McIvor
John Buchan	Callum McSorley
Anne Charnock	Greg Michaelson
Michael Cobley	James Leslie Mitchell (Lewis Grassic Gibbon)
Lyndsey Croal	
T.H. Dray	Ely Percy
Gwyneth Findlay	Rachel Plummer
Gary Gibson	Laura Scotland
Pippa Goldschmidt	Charles Stross
Cat Hellisen	Laura Watts
T L Huchu	Neil Williamson
L.R. Lam	Andrew J Wilson
Katy Lennon	
Caroline Lyndsay	With plenty more writers to come.

If you're a Scottish writer of science fiction, fantasy or speculative fiction, send us your favourite published story, and take your place on SF Caledonia. Nominations also welcome. Details on page page ivpage 127

Theia
Gwyneth Findlay

I was born the same way you were: amid violent collisions in a hot plane of swirling gas, the accretions of our dead elders coming together to form new life. The fabric of my being danced for millennia around a rapidly expanding ball of fusion and flame, forming and crashing and growing anew among billions of bits of other one-day masses, all bound wild and steady in this new sun's orbit.

sfcaledonia.scot/urls/3

Secret Ingredients
Callum McSorley

I'm a line cook. This is how I became a spy: I come from a binary solar system. We don't have what other beings might call day and night. Nor do we measure days like they measure days, or years like they measure years.

sfcaledonia.scot/urls/si

The Worshipful Company of Milliners
T.L. Huchu

For as long as she could remember – one hour +/- – Kitsi had been in the factory. Before that, everything was bleak, blank, the foreboding ultra-darkness of non-existence.

sfcaledonia.scot/urls/wcom

Meet some of our first SF Caledonians

When I Get Younger

Dylan Kwok

As I lie on the gurney in the operating theatre, the nurses potter around. One of them sets out scalpels, chisels and callipers, while another starts up the skin printer, the follicle implant gun, and the laser bone saw.

On the left, on a big screen, there's an unedited photograph of me from three months ago. My eyes look tired. My hair is dyed, but with obviously greying roots.

It's basically a mugshot.

Of course, that's part of their marketing schtick. To make my present self look as grotesque as possible, so I don't get any eleventh-hour regrets about the surgery.

On the right, on another big television, is an image of the girl whom I will become: bright eyed, fresh skin, new hair, looking thirty years younger.

A girl I had almost forgotten once existed.

I close my eyes and recall the long meeting I had with the surgeon and the technical artist to create that image.

Yes, new skin. No, keep my teeth. He'd want them this way. I'm sure. Yes, of course I want new hair. No, no strange coloured follicles. No curly ones either. See this picture where I'm standing with my husband? Yes, make my hair like that again. Eyebrows? Nose? Ears? Yes, fix them as per my old photographs. No, I don't need piercings for my new ears. I didn't wear earrings back then.

A nurse approaches me. "This is just routine, ma'am, but given it's a day surgery and you'll be on anaesthesia, can you confirm the name of the person picking you up later?"

Annette had agreed to give me a ride.

"And her relation to you is?"

We'd been friends for over forty years.

As the nurse walks off, I lean back into the bed, and think about my husband. We'd discussed the operation, of course. Many times.

After all, he'd been the one to suggest it.

A birthday present, he'd said.

He'd promised to take care of everything, but in the end, as usual, he wasn't here today. A business trip had dragged him off last night.

I'll bring back something nice for you, he'd said.

You'd better.

Finally, the anaesthesiologist puts the mask on my face.

As I close my eyes and inhale, imagining the girl I will become, my chest tightens. What if something goes wrong? What if I don't look younger? What if I don't look like how he remembers? What if he doesn't even recognise me?

I slip into unconsciousness.

〰️

They give me an hour to recover before they begin body tests. They prod my skin. I can feel it. They whisper from across the room. I can hear. They run a stick just over my skin, letting it brush over the fine hair of my newly skinned arms and legs.

It tickles.

The last thing they check are my eyes. They had offered, of course, to use my DNA to grow me new ones so I'd have perfect vision again, but I'd declined. I'd read reports that despite using the same DNA, lab grown eyes weren't identical to one's birth eyes. Apparently in the same way the heat conditions of the womb affect how one's fingerprints develop, so it is for eyes, meaning that people with lab grown eyes don't look like they did before.

Online, too, numerous complaints said that even for clients who only gotten new eyes, the change was so stark family members felt they were a different person altogether. I guess it's not just true that eyes are windows to the soul. One's eyes are also intricately linked to one's soul.

So I'd kept my eyes, and when I pass the eye test—that is, get the same degree as before—they hand me back my progressives.

Then Annette comes to pick me up.

She hadn't agreed with my reasons for undergoing surgery, but we've been friends for decades, and she wasn't going to let me down just because we'd disagreed over this.

And true to herself, she asks about the surgery before I even buckle in. About the experience. About how I'm feeling.

I tell her I'm fine. It's true.

As we turn into my driveway she finally asks. "Is he home?"

"Of course. Where else would he be?" I pause. "Would you like to say hi?"

She shakes her head. "I don't want to ruin your moment."

I smile. "Wish me luck."

I step into the house. My father sits alone at the couch watching a show, as he always does in the afternoons since he retired. He turns at the sound of my entrance. For a moment he looks at me without recognition, then he blinks and his eyes light up. "Marie, you're home." Smiling, he switches off the television.

I give a warm smile back. Tears well up in my eyes. "Yes, I am."

He has not recognised me since before Mum died.

He hobbles over on his walking stick. "How was school?"

"Good." I added, "Professor Thurman lectured about antibiotics today."

"Did she? Fascinating, what they teach nowadays." Then, "Are you seeing Bernhard tonight?"

My husband would be touched my father remembers him. "Tomorrow. He's working today."

My father shakes his head. "Always working, that boy. You make sure he takes care of you, okay?"

I smile. "I'll be okay, Dad. He'll be good to me. I know it."

He smiles, and finally he notices the carrier bag in my hand. "What's that? Let me take it for you."

I proffer it to him. "It's a cake, Dad."

"For what?"

"Your birthday."

"My birthday?"

"Yes Dad. Today's the twenty-fifth of July."

I watch my father's face go through a series of emotions: surprise, confusion, delight, then cheekiness. "Oh my, where'd all the years go?" He pats me on the shoulder. "Well, let's get eating before your Mum finds out you got cake, then, shall we?"

I nod, eyes wet with tears.

Dylan Kwok is a Singaporean author and video game designer. His stories have appeared in *Uncharted, Daily Science Fiction, The Colored Lens, Wyldblood, Quarterly Literary Review Singapore,* and *The Best Asian Short Stories 2023*.
You can see more of his work on his blog, 64thopinion.com.

Once Upon a Biofuture: Tales for a New Millennium is an anthology of stories, from fiction to memoir, by a multidisciplinary team of scientists in the UK Centre for Mammalian Biology at The University of Edinburgh

A mix of biology, philosophy and mythology, they explore a powerful new technology that is re-engineering our world: synthetic biology. Many of the stories are biographical, offering insight into how the scientists become scientists and the lessons learned through science exploration, or taking us to new imaginative worlds

The stories were recorded and transcribed, or workshopped and edited by Jessica Fox, former storyteller for NASA, and artist-in-residence at the Centre. This unique role enabled the scientists to lead the storytelling and retain creative control while being guided by an experienced writer.

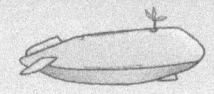

Once Upon a Biofuture: Tales for a new millennium
Edited by Jessica Fox
Published by The New Curiosity Shop/ Shoreline of Infinity Publications
ISBN: 978-1-7396736-6-6
RRP: £12.00

Stories from Science...

...is what happens when you gather scientists and writers together.

To find out more and discuss your ideas visit:

www.shorelineofinfinity.com/storiesfromscience

Available from all good bookshops or direct from:

SHORELINE OF INFINITY

www.shorelineofinfinity.com

DUNDEE

Sunriders

Anna Ziemons-McLean

Eilidh sat soaking up the sun, one hand on the engine of the Steadfast as the little craft rested on the ground. As Suncrafts went, she wasn't the prettiest; somewhat boxy, with a fully backed seat complete with seatbelt and a large storage trunk at the back. She was modelled after an old Vespa, with a focus on comfort, safety and practicality – not that anyone in Eilidh's engineering group seemed to appreciate that.

Blake was late to meet her, as expected, so Eilidh took a deep breath and tried to enjoy the good weather.

"Be more present in the moment," her counsellor's voice said. *"It'll do you some good."*

Eilidh stretched to loosen her muscles. The afternoon was warm and balmy, the air heavy with the musky sweet smell of heather growing up the sides of the Domes. Scotland hadn't had a

Art: Toeken

day this warm in quite a while, though it was well within normal parameters, as Eilidh had been reassured in her session just that morning. The rays bouncing off the solar glass made it feel hotter than it was in the city, and the buildings near the centre of Dundee were almost all glass now, aside from the Domes that made up campus. The Dean had opted for a 'beehive' theme for the remodel, with hexagonal slates paving the paths and planters full of wildflowers dotted around wherever they would fit. The Domes represented the 'hives', full of students working and collaborating together.

In theory.

A familiar figure approached, revving the false engine of her hideous, impractical Suncraft. Blake tossed her dark hair and slid her sunglasses down her nose as she pulled up beside the bench, hovering about a quarter foot off the ground.

Eilidh stood, up and crossed her arms. "Ready to race?"

Blake looked doubtfully at the Steadfast. "It's weird you put fast in the name, but I do admire your optimism."

"That's not what Steadfast means," Eilidh said.

"I know. It's called a joke?"

"You're lucky I even agreed to this," said Eilidh. "Considering yous all went behind my back. I should've just told Alan."

Alan was the head of department for Undergraduate Solar Innovation. He was also the lecturer who had given Eilidh the role of project lead.

Blake pushed her sunglasses back up. "It's called a group project, Eilidh. Group. We couldn't get a word in edgeways."

"Whatever. It doesn't matter. Let's just get this over with. Did you tell Callum where to meet us?"

"Aye," said Blake. "He should be here soon."

Callum McKane was the top student in their class, as even Eilidh begrudgingly admitted. He had agreed to judge the contest, no questions asked, in return for a supersized tofu burrito from the student café – which was lucky for Eilidh, considering her fellow group members were backstabbing traitors.

"Hey!"

They both turned to see Callum running up the path towards them. His face was bright red, his hair damp with sweat. "Hey... sorry I'm late... class ran over. Ooh, are these your crafts?" He bent down. "Can I have a look?"

Blake jumped off her saddle, puffing out her chest. "Sure thing, this is the Hotshot." She gestured to her monstrosity with one hand. "80kw engine, speed of 120 miles per hour, high-def speaker system, and obviously, she's a beaut."

Callum whistled. "I gotta say, she is gorgeous. What's the noise she's making right now?" He ran his fingers over the engine box, then opened it to look inside.

"Oh, we installed a purr. You know, to mimic what an old-fashioned motorbike would sound like. She's actually modelled after a Harley Davidson. My Grandpa used to own one."

"Does she charge as you ride?" Callum asked.

"Ehh... sort of."

Blake gestured to a tiny, almost invisible strip of solar panel along the side of the Hotshot.

"You call that a charging panel?" said Eilidh.

Blake ignored her. "She doesn't actually need to charge that often, because of her backup engine."

"Backup engine?" Callum squinted into the engine box. "Ah! I see..."

"It runs on biodiesel. We might be the sunniest city in Scotland, but that's no saying much. So, I thought it'd be smart to have an alternate power source."

"It's barely even a Suncraft at this point!" said Eilidh. "Have you got any idea how much water making biodiesel uses up?"

Blake rolled her eyes. "Ugh, this is why the group turned against you. You aren't willing to compromise on anything."

"Okay, that's enough." Callum adjusted his glasses. "We're here to compete, not to debate. Eilidh, let's take a look at yours."

Eilidh cleared her throat. "This is the Steadfast. She's completely solar powered and, as you can see, she charges as you ride." Eilidh gestured to the panels lining the front of the bike. "The trunk at the back also folds into a seat for a passenger."

She lifted the back of the seat up and locked it into place. "Under the seat, you will find storage of one cubic foot and because of her suspension, she can carry up to 250kg in weight. For this reason I think the Steadfast could be really useful for emergency services such as paramedics, mountain rescue and the coastguard."

Callum grinned. "Now that's what I call a tank! How's her energy efficiency?"

"Well, because I didn't waste time with speakers or fake engines, her charge can last up to twelve hours of use, provided she isn't going at maximum speed."

"And what's maximum speed?"

"Sixty-five miles per hour."

Blake snorted. "How does that suspension help the emergency services if the patient is dead by the time they get there?"

"You really think they're going to need more that sixty-five miles per hour in the city?"

"Maybe not, but what about the mountains or the sea?"

"Okay, okay, let's have a look at the engine, huh?" Callum knelt down and opened the engine box at the back of the Steadfast. "Wow... this looks intricate. Is it your own design?"

"It is, yes," said Eilidh.

Blake stuck her tongue out.

"How much did it cost to make?" asked Callum.

"It... wasn't cheap," said Eilidh. "But on a larger scale I'm sure there would be ways to make it more affordable."

"Right, okay, I'm satisfied these will both ride fine." Callum stood up and wiped his hands on his jeans. "I had to be sure you weren't going to explode mid-air. I can't be connected to that."

Blake shrugged. "Aye, makes sense. So, what's our first trial?"

"First trial is city navigation. You'll both start at the university and race to Camperdown Park." Callum handed them each a map. "Here are your routes. I ran them through an AI to check that they were each the same length and had the same traffic expectations. Are you both familiar with these roads?"

"Yes," said Eilidh and Blake nodded.

"Good. I'll be riding along the fastest route, so I should get there before either of you do. This trial is going to test the agility and speed of your craft, but please remember to abide by traffic law." He shot Blake a look.

"What? Why are you looking at me?" she asked. "If anything, I'm more likely to abide by traffic law. I've got three points on my craft licence, I can't get another one."

Eilidh huffed through her nose. "I can't believe the group would rather listen to you."

"Maybe you should consider why that is," said Blake "I'll give you a clue, try looking in the mirror…"

Callum clapped his hands. "Right! Are you going to argue all day, or are we going to race?"

Eilidh glared at Blake, then climbed onto the Steadfast and buckled herself in. Blake hopped up onto the saddle of the Hotshot and leaned forward.

"First one to the park without damaging their craft wins this trial." Callum raised his hands. "Okay… three… two… one… go!"

The two crafts lurched forward.

Dread built in Eilidh's stomach as the Hotshot tore ahead and darted off down a fork in the road. The Steadfast had a slow building acceleration, but Eilidh was a much better driver than Blake and Callum had definitely added that damage clause for a reason. The Hotshot was new and unspoilt, but Blake's old Suncraft, a slim electric hoverbike, was covered in dents and scratches. It wasn't just road sense either. She had completely decimated her hoverboard earlier that same term trying to execute a kickflip. Eilidh knew because she was showing off the bruises in class.

Cruising down Perth Road, Eilidh groaned at the sight of a traffic jam up ahead. The whole road was blocked, and the

Steadfast was too wide to fit into the narrow gap between lanes. To incentivise more people to own them, Suncrafts were allowed to manoeuvre in ways other vehicles couldn't, though this wasn't something Eilidh took advantage of often. Up until a year ago, they were even able to fly above traffic, although an unfortunate accident involving electrical cables had left most of Dundee a no-fly zone.

After finally pulling through the lights, the Steadfast gathered speed as Eilidh zipped down the A90. The wind caught the loose strands of hair that escaped her helmet and stuck them to her lip gloss, making her sputter and spit.

"Be more present in the moment."

It wasn't exactly easy advice to follow. Not with every news site posting articles about how they weren't out of the woods just yet. Not with petrol restricted to use by the wealthy and emergency vehicles only. Not with the energy grid unable to support full-scale electric car charging and Suncrafts nowhere near where they needed to be to replace cars.

The temperature of the earth had stabilised, but if they weren't careful, it could increase again next year. For now, new farming methods could support the population, but one bad harvest could send them right back.

As she passed Ninewells, Eilidh felt a tug in her gut.

Her mum had called last Sunday to tell her the news. She was pregnant again, with a little girl. They were going to call her Lilah. When she was younger, Eilidh had always wanted a sister. She had wanted children too. As she had grown older, went to university and made friends, she had changed her mind on that front.

They all agreed, the world wasn't stable enough. But Lilah was coming whether the world was stable or not. She wanted to be excited. She wanted to be the cool older sibling with a degree and a Suncraft design and money for ice cream; but it felt like that was a long way off.

As Eilidh drove further out, the city changed its shape. She was travelling at the exact speed limit, but it was still slow enough that she could appreciate the feeling of space that grew outside of the centre. There was more greenery, more gardens, more vegetable patches since the council had introduced incentives for homegrown food. She wanted to take solace in that. She wanted to hope. She was trying her best; it just wasn't something that came naturally to her.

Riding along the Green Circular, Eilidh heard the rumble of Blake's stupid fake engine. She flattened herself down onto the handlebars, trying to make the craft as streamlined as possible. She sped down the road to the park, flying past blooming bluebells and knapweeds before turning into the car park to find Blake already waiting, leaning against her craft with a shit-eating grin. Callum was stood beside her, a hoverscooter floating at his feet.

"Hey, what took you so long? We were starting to worry…" Blake raised her eyebrows in an expression of mock concern.

"There was a traffic jam. You might want to work on that AI," Eilidh said to Callum.

Callum shook his head. "Nope. There was a traffic jam on Blake's route too."

"I nipped around it." Blake patted the saddle of the Hotshot. "She handles like a dream."

"Oh shut up," said Eilidh

Blake smirked.

"Right, onto our next trial," said Callum. "Each of you is going to ride the Tangle."

"Oh sweet…" said Blake.

The Templeton Tangle was a dirt path running around the woods in Camperdown. Eilidh had ridden parts of the path on her mountain bike as a teenager, but never the whole thing.

"This will test the ability of your craft to withstand rougher terrain," said Callum. "For this challenge I want you to stay at normal altitude, which you would be travelling at over longer distances, even if you weren't in the city. I also want you to stay at the same speed, fifteen miles per hour.

Blake groaned. "Fifteen?"

"Yes. At the end, I will check the state of your bikes, yourselves and your cargo."

"Cargo?" asked Eilidh

"Yes." Calum reached into his backpack and pulled out two cartons of eggs. "Now before you accuse me of food waste, they're already off. So try not to break them, because they'll stink."

Blake took the eggs and popped the Hotshot's saddle up to put the box underneath. The space was tiny, barely big enough to hold it. Eilidh put hers in the trunk on the back of the Steadfast.

"Won't it rattle around in there?" asked Blake.

"Not if I drive steady," said Eilidh.

"Alright." Blake shrugged. "We'll see."

"Okay, both of you on your Suncrafts," said Callum.

Blake and Eilidh climbed onto their crafts and Callum hopped onto his scooter. It was only a short ride down to the woods and the beginning of the Templeton Tangle.

"Now remember, this is not a race," said Callum. "This is about how smooth the ride it, it's about impact threshold and rider safety. Having said that, I will be expecting you to do each of the dips."

"I could do those with my eyes closed." Blake snorted.

"Please don't," said Callum. "Now line your crafts up."

Eilidh pulled up alongside Blake, her hands clenched tight around the handlebars, knuckles white.

"Ready?"

"Yeah." Eilidh gritted her teeth.

She was winning this one.

Whatever it too

"Okay…" said Callum "One… two… three… go!"

They took off along the path, the trees blurring together as they passed. Blake pulled ahead. The Steadfast was still building up speed as the Hotshot hit the first bump. Blake whooped as she soared over and for a moment Eilidh considered upping her speed. But it wasn't a race. She took a deep breath.

"Be present in the moment."

The Steadfast hummed beneath her, the forest smelled like moss and wet grass. Eilidh looked back at the speedometer as it climbed up to fifteen and she dropped down the other side of the bump. Ahead of her, Blake was hitting the rough part.

The Hotshot climbed to the crest of a small hill and clipped the ground, tipping and skidding over it and out of sight as Blake yelled. Eilidh couldn't held grinning as she rode over and saw the Hotshot on its side, with Blake pulling herself out from under it.

"Eilidh!" Blake called out but Eilidh was already off, over the rest of the bumps and down the trail.

By the time she reached the finish, her eyes were streaming from the wind. She hadn't thought to put her goggles on at such a low speed. It was exhilarating though. Maybe that's what it meant, being present in the moment. She unbuckled and stood up, stretching her legs, then checked the eggs in the back.

Not a single crack, and she knew it wasn't a race, but it was nice to finish first. She leaned up against the Steadfast, ready to gloat when Blake showed up.

It was around ten minutes or so before the Hotshot came into view, Callum riding alongside on his scooter. Blake pulled up and jumped off. Callum put a hand on her arm, but she pushed him away. "Why didn't you stop?"

Eilidh's breath caught in her throat as she looked down. The leg of Blake's jeans was shredded. The skin on her calf too, blood soaking the bleached denim red. Eilidh looked away, her face hot. "Like you would have stopped for me."

"Of course I would have! I was pinned under my craft, if you're racing and you get pinned, people are supposed to stop and help…" Blake rubbed her face, smearing dirt over her cheeks. She was shaky, her eyes watering. She lifted the saddle of the Hotshot and handed the battered, stinking box of eggs over to Callum.

He pulled a black bin bag out of the space below his scooter's handlebars and dropped the box of eggs in.

Eilidh chewed on the insides of her cheeks. "It wasn't a race, exactly."

"The rest of the group was right. You know, I said you were just determined… maybe a bit stubborn but not a complete jerk. You really do just care about yourself."

"Listen, I—I think we should call this off." Callum wiped his eggy fingers on his trousers. "I thought this would be a fun little competition, and we'd go get some scran after, but there's clearly more baggage here than I thought, and Blake's hurt so…"

"No." Blake rubbed her eyes and straightened up. "No, we're finishing this. What's the last trial?"

"I'm not telling you," said Callum. "You ought to bandage up that leg."

Eilidh lifted the lid of the trunk and pulled out her first aid kit. "Here."

Blake snatched it out of her hand then got down on one knee and set to work on her injured leg.

"Blake, listen—" Eilidh started.

"I know what we can do." Blake taped a dressing around her calf. "Tell me, how's the Steadfast's altitude?"

"Oh, no," said Callum "No, I am drawing the line, Blake."

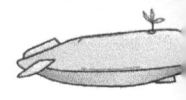

Blake ignored him. "Let's go Sunriding," she said. "You and me, over the Tay."

Eilidh took a step back. "What's Sunriding?"

"We each fly up towards the sun, keeping an eye on our energy levels. The key is to stop when you're at half the charge you started with. Otherwise, you won't have enough to get back down, and you'll drop like a stone."

"A kid died doing that, like, last week!" Callum wrung his hands in front of him. "Come on, can't you just talk this through?"

"So. This is an energy efficiency challenge?" Eilidh asked.

"I suppose you could look at it that way, yeah."

Eilidh folded her arms. "Then I'm fine to ride for it if you are."

"Okay, great." said Blake. "Highest wins."

※

The water on the Tay shone silver under the hot sun. Green hills stretched out on the far shore, dwarfing the small white houses of Newport. The light bounced off a train heading over the Tay Rail Bridge above, wheels clattering against metal. Eilidh hovered opposite Blake, whose brow was set in grim resolve, sweat beading her forehead.

"Please let me talk you out of this," said Callum. "Before someone gets hurt."

He'd been like this all the way down to the shore. Blake hadn't so much as met Eilidh's eyes. Her stomach squirmed.

She should have stopped. She knew that. A person pinned under a craft could have serious injuries, even if it didn't look like a big fall. She'd been about to apologise before Blake suggested Sunriding, which was such a typically stupid, dangerous, Blake thing to suggest.

"Maybe he's right," said Eilidh.

"Chicken, huh?" Blake looked up, making eye contact for the first time since Camperdown. Her expression lacked its usual smugness; she looked sharper, colder.

"No. I'm just thinking about your leg," said Eilidh.

Blake narrowed her eyes. "My leg is fine."

"Alright, great." Eilidh cleared her throat. "Let's ride, then."

"Okay, on the count of three…"

Blake angled the Hotshot skyward and Eilidh followed suit.

"Please, guys…" Callum started.

Blake revved her engine, "One… two… three!"

Eilidh turned her throttle hard and the Steadfast shot up, the rest of Callum's words whisked away in the wind. Rock music blared out from Blake's hideous speaker system as the Hotshot and the Steadfast spiralled around each other, flying up towards the sun.

The glare was blinding even through Eilidh's goggles. The wind pulled at her cheeks and lips and she struggled to tip her head enough to see the energy bar. She'd started at 60%, and she was only at 55% now, even as the clouds soaked her clothes. Blake pulled ahead, her shadow offering Eilidh relief from the sun before she got too far up to see anymore. Eilidh turned her focus to her own craft. This was about efficiency, and if the Steadfast was anything, it was efficient. Even now, it was charging well. The bar was still going down due to the energy it took to maintain altitude, but she had to assume Blake's was going down faster with that puny little charging panel. As the bar hit 50, Eilidh passed Blake hovering in the clouds. Her music was off now and she called out, but again, her words were lost. Eilidh turned the throttle harder with a whoop of triumph. She knew she could stop now, but she wasn't even at 40% yet.

She took in a deep breath. Her lungs felt smaller, constricted. She tried again, but it was like breathing through a straw. Her grip was weak, palms sweating. Her hands slipped from the bars, her head span, and even the adrenaline shock as the Steadfast lurched back couldn't keep her from blacking out.

The wind rushed past. Eilidh struggled to open her eyes as she spun. She couldn't see though the tinted googles, and everything was blurring together anyway. The only thing she was certain of was that she was falling. Her heart felt like a water balloon being squeezed until it popped. She was still strapped into her seat, the Steadfast tumbling, spinning like a fairground ride as she plummeted. She might have been sick if she had enough breath for it.

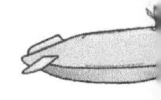

"Eilidh!"

An engine roared beside her. Not the artificial growl of Blake's fake motorcycle purr, something deeper, more guttural, but it was definitely Blake's voice, screaming over the wind. "Eilidh, come on, wake up!"

As the Steadfast tipped the right way up, or at least what Eilidh thought was the right way up, something touched her side and her seatbelt pulled away. For a moment, she was weightless, then what little breath she had was knocked out of her as she was grabbed from behind, still falling, but not as fast. The vibrations of the Hotshot's engine rumbled beneath her and her stomach jolted as her limbs bumped uncomfortably against Blake's.

She went from falling straight down to falling in a curve, slowly straightening out. The Hotshot skimmed the surface of the Tay, sending a salt spray up into the air, before it came to an abrupt stop, jerking Eilidh's neck and almost throwing them both over the handlebars.

Eilidh raised her head. She was awkwardly balanced in Blake's lap, her legs hanging over the edge. Blake's arm was around her back, one hand in a death grip around her shoulder, the other holding the brakes just as tight.

"Eilidh?" Blake's eyes were wider than Eilidh had ever seen them, she was so pale it looked like she might pass out too. "Hey, are you with me?"

Eilidh sat up and vomited over the handlebars. "Sorry," she mumbled.

Blake gave her a tentative pat on the back. "Don't... Don't worry about it."

Eilidh looked over as Blake ran a hand through her hair.

"Hell, did you not hear me yelling at you to stop?"

Eilidh shook her head. "The wind was too high."

"Sorry, I should have warned you, the air gets thin up there," said Blake. "I'm surprised you didn't pass out sooner."

"Guys!" Callum waved as he rode over. "Hey! Hey, is everyone okay?"

"Yeah, she's alright!" Blake shouted back.

"Where's the Steadfast?" asked Eilidh.

Callum pulled up beside them. "Um…" He looked around and his eyebrows shot up. "Oh! It's there!"

The Steadfast bobbed on the water, still seemingly intact.

"There's a rubber ring on the bottom, so it floats," said Eilidh. "Though I suppose it doesn't matter, now." She rubbed her neck. "Blake wins. We'll enter the Hotshot."

"You're thinking about that now?" asked Blake.

"Yeah, aren't you?"

"No! I'm thinking about how you almost died!"

Eilidh flinched at her volume and Blake sighed. "Why does this matter so much to you anyway?"

"I just… I wanted to make something that would help people," said Eilidh. "Something that could carry heavy loads or passengers like a car could. So that when we run out of petrol, things'll be okay. It had to run on solar alone, no biodiesel in case there was a famine or drought. I had to design a whole new engine to give it the necessary power, but you're right. It's slow, and complicated and hard to produce."

"Look, I admire your ambition, but that biodiesel back-up is what saved you," said Blake. "I wouldn't have had the power to do that without it. No solution is perfect. We're all just doing our best, you know?"

Eilidh looked down. Her face flushed hot and her eyes stung. "I just wanted to make something important. I'm sorry I got carried away."

Blake's chewed on her bottom lip "The engine could probably be faster with a few tweaks, and technically, you did win the Sunride. I think we should enter yours."

"You had to save me."

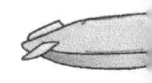

"Aye, but if I cash that in now, I can't hold it over you." Blake smirked, regaining some of her usual demeanour.

"What do you want then?" asked Eilidh.

"I want you to let me fix that engine. And maybe make a couple other changes…"

"No speakers."

"Fine. You're also paying for Callum's burrito."

"And chips," said Callum. "Maybe a can of juice, considering."

"I guess that's fair," said Eilidh.

Blake brought them over to the Steadfast. Eilidh climbed on carefully and fastened her seatbelt. She was still shaking a little, her fingers fumbling with the buckle.

"You okay?" Blake asked.

"Yeah." Eilidh took a deep breath. "Race you to shore, then?"

"Haha, very funny," said Blake.

Eilidh revved the Steadfast's engine and grinned, leftover fear melting away under the hot sun. Blake yelled out indignantly as she took off.

"Oh, oh it's on!" Blake shouted.

Music blared out of the Hotshot's speakers as the two crafts shot across the surface of the silvery Tay, back towards shore.

Anna Ziemons-McLean lives in Dundee and enjoys writing, watching Buffy, and spending time with cats. Anna particularly enjoys writing queer and female-led speculative fiction.

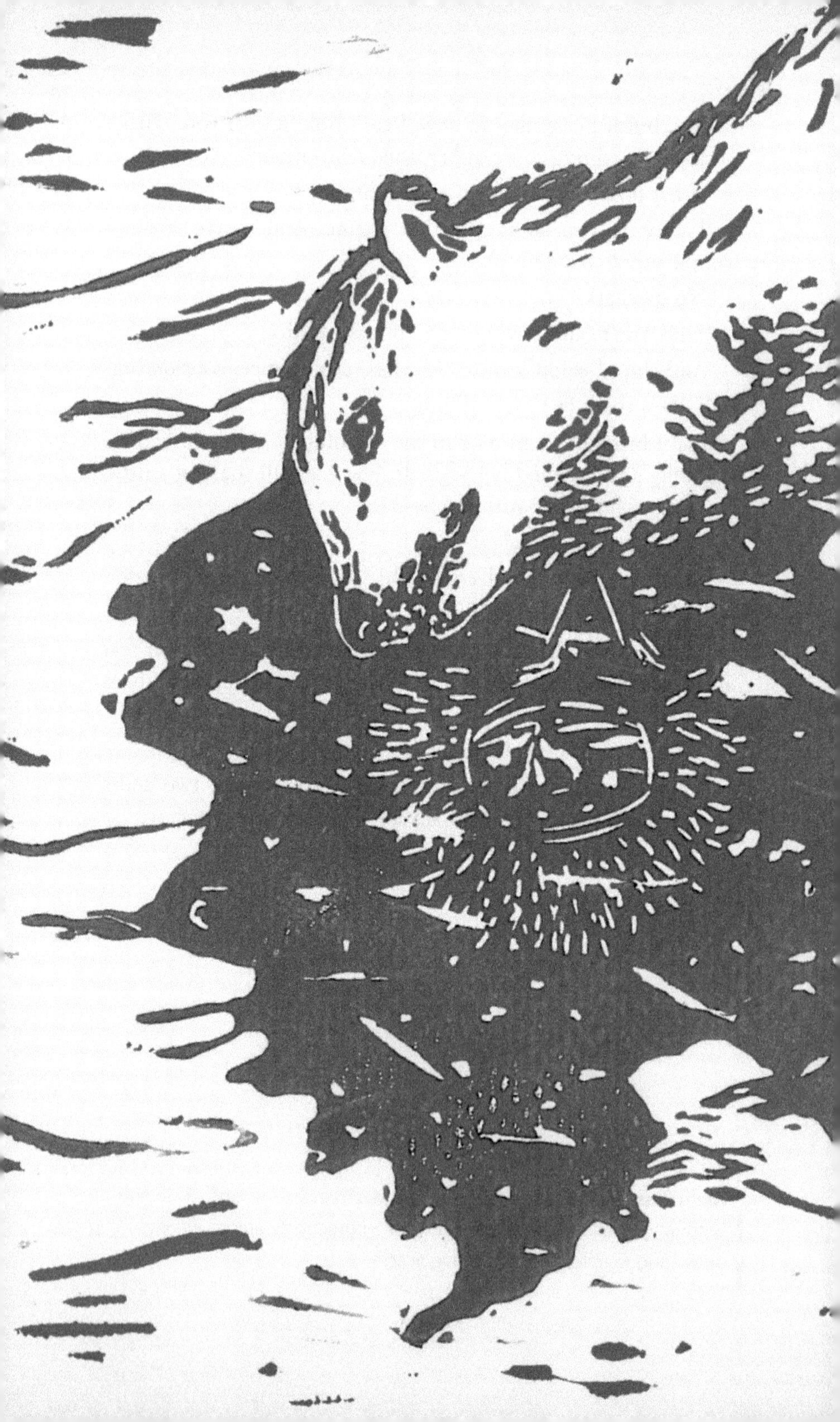

Seed

M. A. R. Rinaldi

Art: C Bennett

Everything is white.

It's only when I raise my head that I see a crimson pattern spread slowly across the snow as the creature collapses. Was it a polar bear? Looked like a fucking polar bear.

Except for the eyes. The eyes looked… human?

"Bravo two-three, are you there? Two-three? Meg?" Pete's voice sounds dim in the cold as it crackles from the radio, fading in and out. "What the fuck happened?"

I take a moment to catch my breath, my eyes still on the creature. "I'm okay. Just got jumped." Sit up, look around, check there are no more. "Can't see a fucking thing out here."

"Jumped? By what?"

"A bear." I think. It's hazy. Even as I reach for the memory of the attack it shifts, just out of reach.

"Did it cut your suit?"

Shit. My suit. I stand up, checking the seals. One of the knee joints is dented, but intact. "No, I'm good. HUD confirming I'm still pressurised. Hang on a second." I tap my helmet but nothing happens. "My main light is down."

"Shit. Forecast … blizzard is here to stay. Do … want to abort?"

I drag my eyes away from the creature, focus on what he's saying. "What? No, no, negative. I'll proceed."

"Is the … okay?"

The word doesn't come out but I know what he's asking. I check my belt. All good.

"Meg," he begins, "Maybe we should abort. We can still—" but I cut him off.

"No! No. You said it yourself. It has to be today. Otherwise…" I trail off. We both know what happens otherwise. There's no time left. "I've still got my wrist torch. That should be enough."

"I still think—"

"I said no." I try to keep the anger out of my voice, but only half succeed. I know he thought the plan was reckless. And even when he agreed, he told me not to volunteer. Begged me. Said I was too close to it. But he doesn't get it; he never did. He's not a parent.

A sigh at the other end. "Your tracker is fading in and out due … borealis. Can you … visual to help us locate you?"

I look around, but everything at ground level is white. I squint, spot something against the shifting luminous hues of the aurora borealis. "I think there's a small crest about a klick away. I'm gonna head that way, maybe see it from there."

A burst of static from the radio before, "… you, okay?"

"Yeah, okay."

I click the radio off and do more checks. The HUD is saying everything is good, but that thing came out of nowhere. Literally. I look around but there are no footprints in the snow. For a moment I put that down to the blizzard, but the indentation I made when it knocked me down is still there. Where the fuck did it come from?

Shake it off, Meg. You have a mission.

Though it's not the mission, so much as the thought of Luke that focuses my mind. For a moment, I think I hear the beeps from the hospital monitor. But that can't be; he's thousands of miles away.

I take a deep breath and check the pressure rifle. A large gouge along the stock, but otherwise it seems in good shape. I pull the lever to load another charge into the chamber.

Before I set off, I can't help but roll the creature over. Its eyes are empty. Black against the white fur. Not human.

You're fucking losing it, Meg.

I look back at the crest, now barely visible. The snow has grown heavier, which I wouldn't have thought possible. I maglock the rifle into the shoulder holster and set off.

It's slow going, but I make it to the bottom in about 20 minutes. Another ten minutes scrambling up, and I'm there.

That's when I see it for the first time. It doesn't look like much, sticking out of the side of the mountain. A small slab of grey concrete extending from the snow maybe 20 metres or so. Easy to miss except for the eerie blue light from the installed artwork above the entrance. Too far to see if the doors are sealed, but the light is a good sign. Means there's still some power.

Might also mean someone else is there.

I try the radio.

"Alpha One, do you copy?" Silence. "Pete?"

After a minute, I give up. Probably not a bad thing. He'd only be a distraction. Try to talk me out of it. Again. I switch my HUD to infrared but nothing lights up.

Go time.

I almost lose sight of it twice in my trek across. Only the pale blue light, flickering through the snow, keeps me on target. I'm about a hundred metres away when I get the sense of something watching me.

I spin round, infrared back on, searching for something, anything moving in the snow. Nothing. Only my own tracks, which are quickly being filled in by the blizzard. Rather than reassuring me, it only makes my heart beat a little faster. I feel the hairs on the back of my neck standing up and pull out the pressure rifle again. I unclick the safety and raise it so I can peer through the sights. Slowly, I circle round again.

My heart stops.

I swing the rifle back an inch, but there's nothing there.

But there was. There was something there.

No, not something.

Someone.

Maybe fifty metres away. Someone had been there. And they looked like…

That's impossible, Meg.

But even as I think it, I'm vaguely aware of my suit monitors beeping as I black out.

✳

"Mom?"

The voice seems distant at first, and it takes me a moment to rouse. The sterile, antiseptic smell of the room hits me first, reminds me where I am. Why I'm here. I open my eyes slowly, thinking it's still daytime, but the only light is from the too-bright LEDs above Luke's bed.

I smile and shift in my seat, trying to act like I had only dozed off. Lean forward and take his hand, careful not to bump the stent.

"Hey, baby, how you doing?"

My son attempts a weak smile, but I can see that even that effort takes a lot. "It's sore."

I stand, moving closer. "I know, baby. I know."

"Did it work?"

The bluntness of the question shouldn't surprise me; of course he wants to know. But I'm still not really prepared for it. Or rather, not prepared how to answer.

"They got a proper look at it all," I manage, attempting a smile.

He gives a small nod, but I see the disappointment in his eyes. No, not disappointment. Acceptance. Acceptance that he will die soon and there's nothing that he can do about it.

Except that I'm not ready to accept it. How could any parent? Does he not realise he's everything to me? And that there is nothing—nothing—I won't do to try to save him.

"It's okay, Mom." He's always known what I'm thinking. That's the connection we've always had, through good times and bad.

And God knows there's been a lot of bad recently.

I feel my eyes growing wet and try to blink the tears away. "It's not okay, baby. It's not okay." I hug him tightly. Holding his frail body takes me back to when he was a young and had fallen. When I told him not to worry and promised him I would do anything to protect him.

You don't break a promise. I told him that.

I step back, my hands sliding to his. I don't try to wipe away the tears. "There's still a way."

"But the doctor said—"

"I know. But I know where I can get it. And I will. I promise."

"Mom…"

I look him in the eye. "I promise."

He gives a sad smile, nods. I lean forward and kiss him. I hope it's not the last time.

As I leave, he says one final thing. "Mom, everything will be okay if you let go."

Then the tears come.

❋

"— two three? Meg?" Pete's voice seems to fill the whole world in that moment. "Meg, do you copy? We're getting alarming readings from your suit."

I let out a breath I hadn't realised I was holding in. "Copy Alpha one. I'm here." I sweep the gun around, looking for tracks. Looking for him. But there's nothing. "I just slipped but I'm good."

"Thank God. Thought we'd lost you there." For some reason he wasn't cutting out anymore. "What's your position?"

"I'm a hundred metres from the door." I'm still scanning slowly around, trying to find that figure, but they're gone. If they were ever there.

"You okay? You sound—"

I cut him off before he can tell me how I sound. I know how I sound. "I'm fine. I think that polar bear just took the wind out of me earlier."

"You sure your suit's okay?"

"Yeah, yeah. It's fine." I check the HUD again anyway. "All fine." I lower the rifle and look at the target. The pale blue light of the artwork faintly illuminates the small metal bridge leading to the main structure. "I'm heading in."

"When you go in there, we lose you."

"I know."

"Just get in, get to the vault, and get out, okay?"

"Roger that."

There's a moment's silence before Pete begins to talk again. "Meg, just be careful, okay? We're not getting any readings from Vault Three."

That's not good, I think, but instead I say, "It'll be fine."

"Meg…"

I know what he wants to say. What he wants me to say. But I can't. Not after what I just saw. Who I just saw. "I'm going in now. Speak to you on the other side. Bravo two-three out."

I click the radio off before he can say anything else. I need a clear head.

A sense of déjà vu washes over me as I approach, despite having only seen this on screen before. The whole entrance structure is only just wider than the double doors that sit underneath the glowing blue artwork. It didn't need to be anything more, of course; this outer structure was purely functional. The real prize was inside the mountain itself.

I'm at the small bridge leading to the doors when I realise that the left-hand door is open. It's not moving, the snow build up has seen to that, but there's a gap between it and the right-hand side.

I pause, trying to think who could have done this. The only people with access to the vault are the two leading Agri-corps. Been that way since the floods. Apart from anything else, there's no way anyone could reach Svalbard without bumping into our guys or NutriTech's. And even if they somehow did, there's no way they could break in. The doors are six inches of solid steel.

Then who did you see in the snow?

No one, I tell myself. I bring up my HUD, check the time. 05:20. Makes it nearly five hours since my shot. I hadn't believed the stories about the hallucinatory effects of the peninsula, but what else could it be? The déjà vu, the bear. The ghost. The doc said that the shot should keep the effects away for at least eight hours. Unless I do have a leak. Maybe that bear did mess with my suit after all. Or maybe it's the borealis fucking with things.

Whatever the explanation, all the options are more rational than seeing someone out here. Than seeing Luke.

But if the shot is wearing off it means I have even less time. I grip the pressure gun tighter as I approach the door. Check the locks.

Shit.

No one has broken in. But someone—something?—has broken out. The metal is buckled from the inside, as if there was an explosion. Only there's no black scarring from a blast.

I reach out a hand to touch it, as if that might tell me something. All it does is confirm how heavy the door is. Light flickers intermittently from the other side of the door. Power's on, but not stable, at least not to the lighting circuits. The display for the electronic lock on the door is busted, doesn't light up when I swipe my wrist over it.

With some effort, I squeeze my way through the small gap. I panic as my bent knee joint catches in the door, but a twist and pull and I'm inside.

I quickly raise my rifle, sweeping an arc around the entrance room which flickers in and out of darkness. Apart from some melting snow that has blown in through the open door, nothing seems out of place.

The inside matches the outside in its ordinariness. A small, narrow room with whitewashed walls. The loud thrum of the cooling systems fills the air. It could have been the backroom to any storage facility in the world. It's just that this one held the key to humanity's survival.

Or its destruction, I think, glancing back at the busted entrance.

There are three doors leading out of the room, but I'm only interested in one.

Apart from the entrance door, there's no sign of anyone else being here.

I pause, wondering if I should try and close the door and then realise I've had this thought before. Or I think I have. The déjà vu is growing stronger. Is it because of the vault? I physically shake my head and force myself to focus. Spend time closing the broken door or keep moving? The systems seem to be working but could a breach put the seeds at risk? No. The inner doors are the important ones; if they're breached, it's already too late. Besides, I'm only here for one batch. The ones that can save Luke.

Stay on target.

I walk across to the middle door and see that the lock panel is offline. I swipe anyway, but nothing happens. But if the outer door is breached...

I pull and it swings open easily. I can now see the lock mechanism has been broken, snapped like a child's toy.

Or a bone.

The tunnel beyond is dark. Lights should kick in as I move down, but then, the door should also be locked. I hold up the rifle and peer through its sights, infrared on. Nothing registers.

Maybe it was the bear, I try to tell myself. Maybe whatever it was is already gone.

But I don't believe it.

The lights do kick in as I make my way along the tunnel, turning on as I approach and off as I continue forward along the 430ft corridor. I keep the rifle raised anyway, doing a narrow sweep back and forth as I slowly make my way forward.

I see them when I'm halfway down the tunnel. The figure barely registers on the infrared sensors, which means they're either dead or dying.

NutriTech, I assume. I stop in my tracks, grip the pressure rifle more tightly. "Hello? Who's there?"

No response.

I take a couple of steps forward, lighting the corridor closer to the hunched figure, try again. "State your name and company."

This time I see the chest heave. Maybe hear a wheeze as well. The figure isn't holding a weapon that I can see so I risk moving closer.

That's when I see the blood. It's pooled around them, thick, red. Already freezing. A large gash across her chest—it is a her, I see now—tells me where the majority of it is from. And then I see she's not wearing the purple-trimmed suit of NutriTech, but the green and black trimmed suit of GaiaWorks. Of my company.

What the fuck?

A huge wave of déjà vu washes over me, so strong that I actually stagger back. Like I've seen this before. Except...

No. That's impossible.

I carefully step forward and crouch down before her.

Before *me*.

Her face is bruised and bloody behind the shattered visor, but the woman looks like me.

Not looks like. *Is*.

I'm looking at myself. Or a version of me.

My HUD is scanning her/my vitals while I take all this in. She's critical. There's no hope for her.

A small movement of the head, another wheeze.

"How...?" I can't even begin to work out how to ask what I need to ask. Instead, I focus on more practical issues. "What happened? What did this to you?"

She opens her mouth to speak, but no words emerge, just more wheezing.

I try to think what could have done this. The gash is large. The bear?

"Was it a bear? Did it follow you in?"

The edges of her mouth curl up slightly. "No, not follow," and it sounds so fucking weird to hear my own voice. "Inside."

"Inside? It was already in here?" My hands tighten around the rifle. I glance around. "There's something in here?"

Her head falls again, her breathing becoming slow.

"Hey!" I lift her head. "Hey, stay with me. How did you… or how did I…"

Her vitals start to crash.

"No, stay with me! Please." I clutch her helmet, try to get her to look at me, but I can feel the life draining away from her.

But then one bloodshot eye finds mine, her hand clutching my belt to pull me closer. She butts her helmet against mine. "Inside."

I pull back, trying to understand.

All she says is, "Everything will be okay… if you let go."

Then she's gone.

I feel a void open inside me as I let go of her. Of me. The déjà vu… is this why? Have I already done this? Already failed?

The scream fills the corridor, echoing off the thick walls. It doesn't sound human. But it doesn't sound like any animal I've heard either. I swing the rifle round, trying to locate its source, but the tunnel falls back into the sound of the constant dull power hum.

"What the fuck was that?" I ask myself, but then I catch sight of dead me again. For a second, I think she's grinning, but then she's not. Her eyes are blank. Like the bear's. No, the bear was just a dead bear. She's just a dead… me.

Get a grip, Meg.

Luke. Focus on Luke. Get the seeds.

I take a deep breath and stand up. The tunnel ends in 50 feet, the door to the vault antechamber lit now. I can already see the lock panel is busted, but that doesn't surprise me anymore.

Vault 2. In and out. You can do this.

The antechamber lights are already on, probably because the door is registering as open. The thrum of cooling and power is louder in here, amplified by the acoustics of the wide-open hall. The entrances to the three vaults sit on the wall opposite, giant metal structures constructed decades ago. The doors to vaults 1 and 2 are sealed, still packed under foot-thick ice. That's where they keep the seeds.

Then I see Vault 3.

It sits open. The floor in front is covered in fractured blocks of ice, broken off from the door when it was opened. It shouldn't be like that. Proper procedure would see the temperature of the door raised, the ice drained off. This is like something wrenched it open. Or broke it open from the inside.

Out of instinct, I try my radio even though I know it will never work this deep into the mountain. I'm greeted only by the hiss of static.

On my own, then. I hope.

I walk across carefully, my HUD scanning constantly for movement or signs of life. As I near, I see the dents on the door. They're from the inside. No creature on Earth should be able to dent these five-foot thick doors.

No creature *from* Earth, I correct myself.

My mind flicks back to the briefing. Pete taking me to the side afterwards. "Even NASA don't know what it is they found up there."

The logos of various space agencies are painted on the outside of the vault door. NASA, ESA, RSA. Space debris locked in a mountain in the artic archipelago ever since the Artemis missions kicked off back in the twenties. Sure it seemed like a good idea at the time. What could go wrong at -68° C?

Evidently, quite a lot.

I raise my rifle as I round the door. I find myself praying—me, praying! Luke would love that!—that there is a rational explanation. An explosion from inside the vault maybe. Perhaps one of the minerals they found is unstable at freezing temperatures, like hexaferrum.

Explain the entrance then, Meg. Explain dead you.

Before I can argue with myself, I see the inside of the vault. No explosion, but something has made a hell of a mess. What's left of the shelves are strewn all over the inside of the vault. Twisted and bent metal lies everywhere. Smashed boxes and lunar samples scatter the ground.

My HUD lights up, warning me my heart rate is spiking.

No shit.

If that thing has already escaped… I lower my rifle, try to think.

Whatever this is, it doesn't matter. I need the seeds. Save Luke, then worry about whatever this is. As soon as I'm out, I can radio Pete. Hell, I can send out an SOS, get NutriTech here as well.

As long as I have the seeds.

Given the state of the rest of the facility, I'm surprised to find the controls for Vault 2 operational. It takes maybe an hour to go through the steps to open the door, but I feel my heart leap when it does.

I step into the vast space which is filled with shelves and containers. Fortunately, I know where I'm going. Row 3, Shelf 3. Easy.

For a moment, I think the container is missing, but it's just shifted slightly, hidden behind another one. I pick up the box and stare at the name on the label.

Artemisia absinthium L.

Hard to believe that these are the only seeds in existence. That they could be grown into something that could save Luke.

"Everything will be okay if you let go."

His last words to me echo in my head. Doesn't he realise I can't? That I made a promise, and you don't break promises.

It's when I turn to leave that the door to the antechamber explodes towards me.

I fall backwards, shelves around me collapsing, seeds spilling everywhere.

I panic, realising my hand is empty, the seeds gone.

It's when I sit up that I see it.

At first, it's a bear-like creature, but in the blink of an eye, it shimmers and shifts, as if trying to find a form that suits it. A man. The figure seems featureless at first, but as it locks eyes with me, it transforms again. I realise it's not trying to find a form that suits it. It's trying to find a form that suits me.

It becomes Pete.

I think of dead me butting helmets with me. "*Inside.*"

I realise now that the reports of hallucinations began shortly after the first Artemis mission. Has it been here all this time?

He smiles as he approaches, his grin too wide.

"Hey, Meg." It even sounds like him.

I scramble backwards, pull my rifle. Try to let off a couple of shots.

Click.

Fuck.

He's close now, even as I stand and step backwards, only to find a fallen shelf behind me. I shift round, getting another shelf between me and him.

"You're not going anywhere, Meg."

It reaches out but I pull back, press myself as hard as I can against the shelves. The thing's head tilts, morphs again.

Into Luke.

"Mom, I need you." It sounds so much like him I almost leap forward to hug him. Instead I say, "Fuck you."

Luke's features frown and its hand grasps forward even more, inches from my suit. I feel my breath quicken as its fingers turn into points, its hand becoming a bulging mass of shifting veins.

"I need to be you." This time the voice doesn't sound like Luke. It doesn't sound human at all.

Why me, I think. Then realise it needs a form it can pass for when it leaves here. My God, what if it leaves here?

A beeping from my HUD interrupts my thoughts.

"Countdown ten seconds."

What the fuck? I glance down at my belt and with horror, see the numbers ticking down on the face. The contingency GaiaWorks build in. That we all have to sign a waiver for, to prevent company secrets falling into the wrong hands. But why is it ticking?

Then I remember Dead Me pulling me close with my belt.

I grab it, holding the pause switch, stopping the numbers at one second temporarily.

My eyes fall on the seeds scattered around me. I see the packet of Artemisia seeds now. Right at my feet. I think of my last conversation with Luke. Of my promise. His last words to me...

The same words Dead Me said.

I look at the seeds then at the bomb in my hand, my fingers gripping the pause switch.

Everything will be okay if you let go.

The creature growls, the shelf buckling as its claws reach me.

I close my eyes, think of Luke.

And I let go.

Everything is white.

M.A.R. Rinaldi is a Scottish-Italian writer of speculative fiction living in Edinburgh, Scotland. He also writes historical fiction and thrillers under Marco Rinaldi, and is represented by Francesca Riccardi of Kate Nash Literary Agency. In addition, he is co-host of the popular "Page One - The Writer's Podcast", in which he interviews writers of all kinds about their writing process.

The 2024 Cymera Festival/ Shoreline of Infinity Short story competition for Scottish writers brought out a fine bunch of tale tellers from all over the world.

Winning story:

Forgetting is Their Word for Death
by **Paul McQuade**

Runners up:
Eagles
by **Iain Bain**
The End of the Line
by **R/L Monroe.**

Congratulations to all three.

We had a startlingly brilliant shortlist to pick from, so everyone here can be smugly proud for their efforts:

Katya Bacica
Laura Borrowdale
Sam Healy
Anja Hendrikse Liu
Ian Hunter
Anne McClure
May Bird
Casey Peterson
Anna Rickards
Cal Rosie

We invited two of our favourite writers, Pippa Goldschmidt and Camilla Grudova, to be the judges, and they dove deep into the task. Here are their reports:

Camilla Grudova:

The high quality of the shortlist made narrowing down to just three stories hard, but left me exuberant and optimistic for the future of speculative fiction in Scotland.

In *Eagles*, rare wildlife has 'invaded' Glasgow and eagles are dismissed with the same annoyance we give to seagulls. It is a topical and dark-humoured story.

The End of the Line, mixing workplace commentary with science fiction depicts the hilarious effect of a rude, high maintenance restaurant customer undoing a whole society with her demanding requests, a story I could relate to having worked in many customer service jobs.

Forgetting is Their Word for Death is a Ballardian tale set in the far off future, the awakening of someone, sleeping beauty style, who gradually remembers they volunteered to be preserved for future use. The author's love of and skill with language is evident, and I took great delight in such lovely lines as "Largely shapeless, bald, the nose, ears, and eyes worn down by time to a protean mass. A homunculoid people. My descendants."

Pippa Goldschmidt:

The shortlist of 13 stories made a fantastic read, with huge variety of subject matter and writing styles. The stories transported us from the streets of Glasgow to the far reaches of the Universe - via hospitals, restaurants, forests and space stations.

Not surprisingly several stories imagined the effect of climate catastrophe on our world, others riffed off the social implications of imagined technologies.

As ever in science fiction, dystopias were a common theme, but treated very differently.

Eagles was a deserved runner-up with its depiction of wild animals invading Partick, providing a surreal backdrop to everyday life.

The End of the Line was a humorous example of the butterfly effect – a restaurant order going awry might spark the end of civilisation.

Forgetting is Their Word for Death is a beautifully written sad and elegiac tale on the importance of language in navigating the natural world, and a warning of what might happen to humanity if we allow that world to disappear.

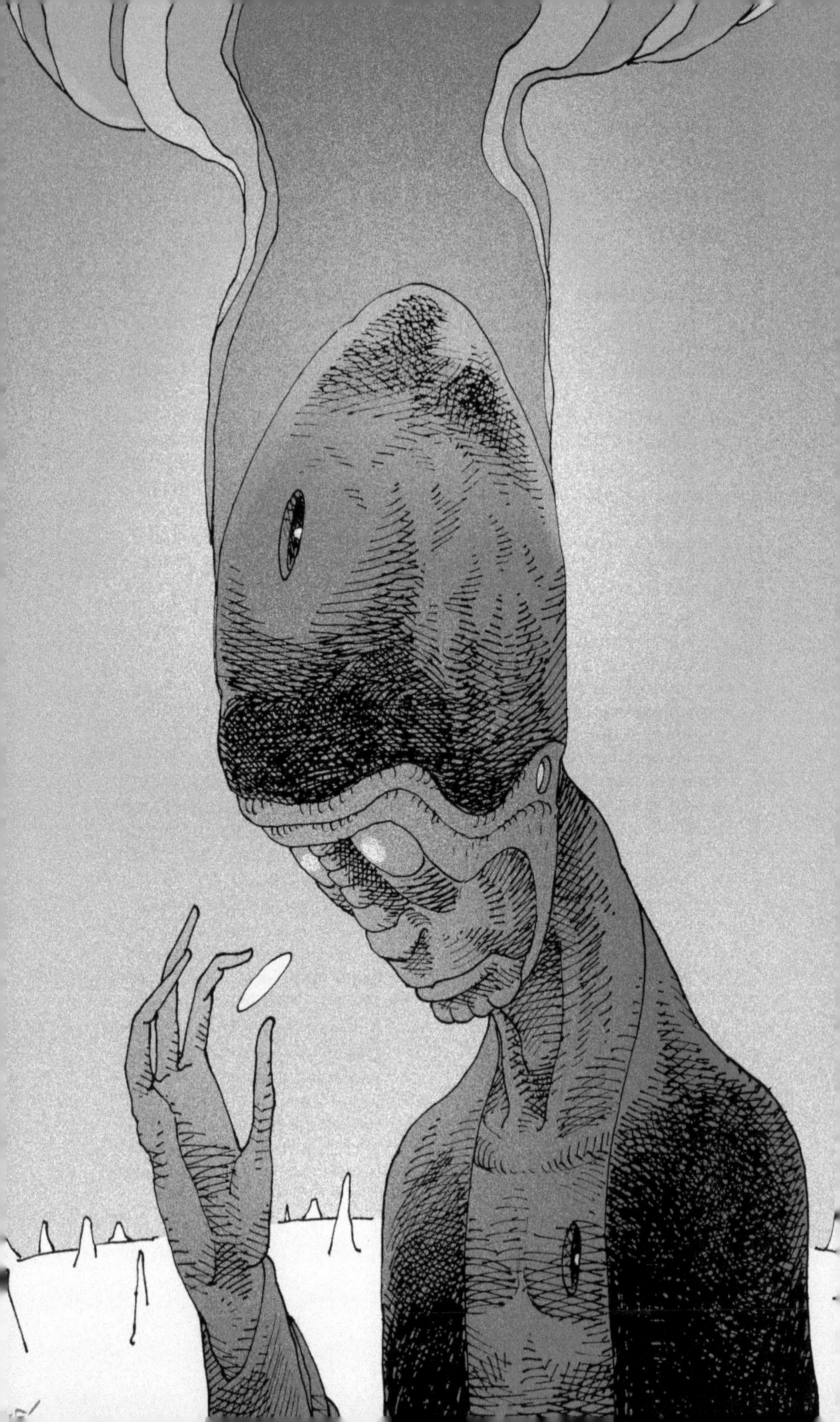

Winning story of the Cymera Festival/ Shoreline of Infinity short story competition 2024

Forgetting is Their Word for Death

Paul McQuade

Translation recovered from site 18554, "Pressmennan Wood". No copy of original found. Most likely machine translation.

An awakening is no small thing. So many mechanisms move and shift to put the mind in place, say, *here, now, this moment*. It is only when something pours turpentine in this frame of reference that we see things as they are. Autobiographic memory returns first, when waking, but I woke that morning with none. I lay there, and the where, the why, the who, failed to cohere. I simply was: in a bed, a room without windows, alone.

Art: Stref

Someone entered the room then. The way they held themselves, the words they used, were familiar but not recognisable. The muffled sound of a conversation in another room. They wore colours I wouldn't put together, white, blue, medical, I thought. A doctor, maybe? But no doctors I knew wore veils like this. The features were indistinguishable beneath. The voice told me nothing of the gender of the speaker. But the words. In them I thought I sensed some echo of home.

'Where am I?' I asked.

The figure stopped, cocked its head, as though listening to another voice, then spoke. They were not immediately intelligible. I pieced it together primarily through syntax. That and the word *Pressmennan*.

The figure pointed at a vase on a sidetable. The flowers were, like the figure's language, familiar though not recognisable. Some blue flowers may have been bluebells but were far too large. Primrose and sprigs of larch, but again, distorted. Scale, variegation in colour. It was not just that they were *wrong*. That would have been easier. It was that they were familiar *and* wrong. Like a stranger wearing the face of an old friend.

'Flowers,' I said, in an attempt to end the interaction. Again, that cocking of the ear to a distant voice.

'Names,' it said.

'Larch,' I said by instinct. 'Primrose. Sycamore. Bluebell.'[1]

A word bubbled up in my head as I spoke: *deixis, the function of pointing or specifying from the perspective of a participant in an act of speech or writing.*

I knew these technical terms better than the names for flowers. But as for the centre, the who I am, that remained absent. Not forgotten but excised. I was a topic without subject, a pointing without pointer. But why?

I allowed myself to be led out of the bedroom. I hesitate to use the word *cell*, considering the ample furnishings, private

---

[1] Archival note: Translation software has not preserved these terms. Exact nature of specimen's language remains unknown.

bathroom, and *objets* whose nature eluded me. But I could only breathe when this person led me out of that place, through a circular corridor, and into a central space dominated by the largest specimen of *pinus sylvestris* I had ever seen. Scots fir. A dome of glass sheltered it though with no visible join. Beyond the glass was fog, dull, iron-grey. At the base of the tree were flower and vegetable beds, equipment, computers: everything translucent, barely there.

My attendant spoke to me in that strange language. It gestured for me to follow it through the garden to a circle of stones, moss-covered, on which sat three more attendants like itself. Their clothing was shapeless, and over their heads, all wore the hooded veil. It seemed to be a laboratory artefact rather than a cultural one. Another figure walked toward me, pulled me down on a rock, and presented a length of clear material on which I could see images.

I recognised this immediately. A language gathering exercise. They were trying to draw out my language so they could document it. Does my language distinguish men from women, does it distinguish one from five, does it use different words for the living and the dead?

I felt relieved. I had no idea who I was but this, at least, I knew. All I had to do was narrate the images.

The first was simple: A person of indiscriminate gender is planting seeds. In the next, they are reaping wheat, the next, bailing. Then finally drinking with friends under a harvest moon. So far so good.

There was a sphere. The planet. Suspended in a substance that didn't look like the blackness of space but the same grey as the fog outside. I tried my best to explain what I saw.

In the next, a tear across the planet's surface. Something was emerging from it. This proved much harder. When I struggled, one of the researchers leaned forward and said: *Monster. Evil.*[2] I nodded. I understood, now. I did not tell them that it looked,

---

2   Archival note: No record of this field study has been found.

from a different angle, like germination.

Next slide.

'Something evil was born,' I said. 'It destroyed everything.'

Next slide.

'This is what is left.' I looked in dismay at an image of a dome, in the centre of which was a Scots fir.

'Understand now,' the one who had spoken before said, in my language.

'More,' another said.

'What's outside this place?' I asked, pointing to the fog.

They looked at each other, then one answered. 'Forgetting,' they said.

✣

I was taken to the storyboards multiples times. They kept me there, in that room, and then led me away. The light remained constantly dimmed in the rooms and bright in the garden. I could not think of it in circadian rhythm.

I asked to leave the cell. I asked for food. They brought me tea, dishes that might be small cakes but denser, savoury, and vegetal. They ignored my requests for autonomy. The most they give me was the word: 'Calibrating.'

My one solace was that I convinced them to give me materials to write with. More documents, more language for them to harvest. The saddest thing is that it is here, in the language exercise, that I feel most myself. As though only then am I fulfilling my purpose.

It took a while for me to realise what about the storyboards had struck me as odd. They had not yet produced a mirror. Every surface in this place was matte. Even the great dome held no reflection. But I had expected them to show me a mirror, to be asked to narrate myself, to say who I was in my language. They didn't.

It was as if they understood what I was still trying to understand. It was not retrograde amnesia - I knew and remembered plenty, especially concerning language. No. I was missing the deictic centre, the observational self. They knew. And they didn't care.

I did not hate them their coldness. My captors, 'the researchers', always in their medical garments, leading me through their images, the end of their world. I was far more repulsed by my own urge to help them, an impulse that felt foreign to me even as it moved me to speak. I felt no threat from the researchers. Their way of being in this place was more pathetic than deadly. And yet they held the keys to my prison.

※

I have no idea how many cycles of images before I could procure an access key. How many times had the world ended before I managed to remove one from an attendant? They searched the room and my person. Of course they did. I had secreted it in the garden where anyone might have dropped it. So many cycles of apocalypse before I made the attempt to explore my prison.

It is true that there is no light and day, here. But there is a rhythm to the movement of the researchers. A time when the majority of them are occupied elsewhere. You can feel it in the breath of the place, like clockwork winding slowly down

I wasn't looking for anything in my escape beyond the thrill of being unattended. My first forays into doors of the torus were met with rooms like my own. Some doors didn't open. These I took to be exits. I could not leave this place of my own accord. But then, seeing the door, thinking of the grey behind it, I saw the images of calamity. I was safer in the dome. There was nothing outside but forgetting.

An uninspiring labyrinth. It was only as I turned a corner and saw one of the researchers emerging from a room that I thought it might not be in vain. I went in after it, down a set of stairs, carved in stone, and into the first true dark I had seen since awakening.

A circular room, vaulted, veined with the roots of the great fir. The walls were lined with columbaria. Inside, documents in a language I could not read, but I recognised the genome sequences, the hyperspectral imaging. A seed bank. That's what this place was after all, it seemed. In these, nothing so extraordinary. Simply the hope of a people who wanted, one day, to be able to plant their seeds again.

But in the others.

Spheres, jade green, marbled, so that in each it seemed there lived a whole cosmos. I could not bring myself to touch them. The revulsion was primal. My organs spoke to me. To touch them would be to violate something older than law. I left them, not quite understanding why or what they were, until I came across a columbarium with a hollow sphere.

Again, that language I could not read. But an image. It took me a moment to recognise myself, so starved of surfaces and reflections. But it was me. This box. And I understood, then, how I had come to be regrown here. What I had volunteered myself for so many years ago.

I was a repository of data. A kind of hard-drive made out of a person. The infinite plasticity of the mind, surpassed, at no point, by any of those devices claiming to mimic the neural net. This is why I was here. And why I was empty. The deictic centre had been removed to make way for other things, for words like *primrose, eventide, calamity*. Looking at this, I knew I had agreed to it myself, and I could tell, without being able to read it, that the sign above my tomb read: *Last native speaker.*

☙

I made my way back without incident. I cannot adequately detail what I felt. Lonely. Yes. The weight of the realisation that I was the last of my own people. But my sadness was not for me; a small part, yes, but the greater was for them. For the researchers, the conservationists, my captors, my resurrectionists.

I understood them more, working with them, knowing the seed bank, the repository, all the souls they kept in this place. They are waiting for the day when what they have conserved will be of use. It is clear that they brought me back, if I can call it that, as part of that mission. Only, they have forgotten what it is they were trying to save. They cannot even name their loss.

They want me to walk the garden and give them the names for all the things they have forgotten now. They have no ghosts to haunt them, they have no pain to feel; they are a people cut off from everything that made them a people. They live. They are lifeforms. They remember their purpose, maybe, though that seems instinct now more than anything. They are so much sadder to me than anything I could imagine. They know so much and they know nothing. They know preservation without love, life without heart. They know only the sadness of unhaunted places. And I pity them this above all else.

I went through the charade to keep them happy. I told them the story of their world and how it ended. They gathered the words like seeds. Then I stopped. I made them a bargain.

'I will continue with this,' I said, 'on two conditions. I want you to tell me why you are doing this. Not what your mission is. *Why*.' I hoped their 'calibration' had allowed them to understand the nuance of my question. 'And I want to see you unveiled.'

Much conferring. Outside the fog was still and blank and grey as malice.

The veil came off like a beekeeper's veil; connected by a seam to the hood at the back. The fine mesh had not hidden much. Largely shapeless, bald, the nose, ears, and eyes worn down by time to a protean mass. A homunculoid people. My descendants.

It was as I suspected. The end of their world was the end of my own future, the end of everything we had sought to prevent. And yet we had saved a part of a part of a part. Was that enough? Looking at the shapeless face, it did not seem to be.

My attendant placed their hands on mine and drew me to look at the dome and the fog. This was its answer to the question. *Why?*

'Forgetting,' it said.

I tried my best not to cry.

I admire them and I loathe them, the researchers. They save and they save and they save and they do not know why or for whom or what it might mean to save something for the love of it. They know only life. They think life itself is enough.

I cannot give them the words that will help them understand the monstrosity of this.

We have exhausted the storyboards, I think. The researchers are unsure what to do. They seem restless, too, as though something is coming they can sense but not understand. I want to leave. I have passed on what I must and now I am left, this hollowed out thing, regrowing what I had lost – the sense of myself. Though what use that might be in a ruined world I have no idea. My mission is accomplished at least. Maybe now it is time to be more than simply a living archive.

To whoever finds this message, my language is preserved here, in this place. But I am somewhere else. I have left Pressmennan Wood. One way or another. I have to leave this place. I have to face what the researchers here cannot face: all that has been lost, piled up at the door. The many, many deaths beyond measure. The simple horror of forgetting. I have to leave. I have to see what can be rebuilt, whether or not the seeds of this place can still be planted. Whether there might still be hope. For me. For you. For us.[3]

---

[3] Archival note: No other documents have been recovered from the ruins of site 18554. Specimen's language is thus considered extinct.
End of document.

Paul McQuade is a writer and translator originally from Glasgow, currently based in Upstate New York.

His writing has received the Sceptre Prize for New Writing, the Austrian Cultural Forum Writing Prize, and been shortlisted for both the Bridport and White Review short story awards. He is the author of the short story collection Between Tongues.

His website is: www.paulmcquade.com

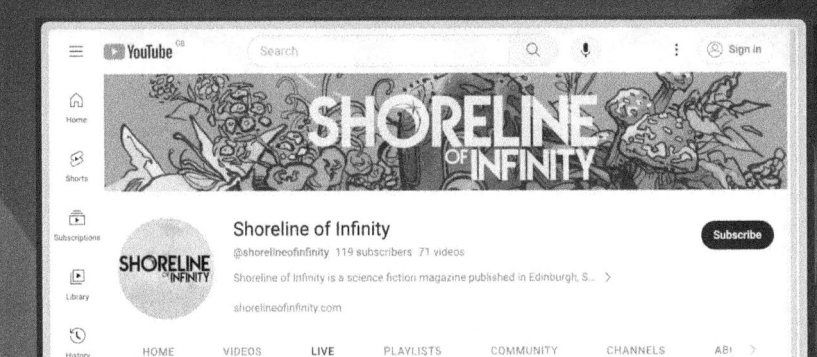

Shoreline of Infinity's Event Horizon: live, online and on Youtube.
www.youtube.com/@shorelineofinfinity

NOISE AND SPARKS

Ruth EJ Booth

Goodbye to All That

With apologies to Joan Didion (and by extension, Robert Graves).

Despite my incredulity, in two months and less than an hour's walk from where I'm currently writing, Glasgow Worldcon 2024 will be kicking off. For fledgling authors outside the US and London, a Worldcon in your own backyard is a magical thing, akin to the Goblin Market of publishing. *Finally*, thinks the writer, *the industry has come to me*. Perhaps they've had a few stories published before or been to the odd convention – but this is something new. The editors and overseas publishers they've longed to work with, the big-name writers they've admired, all in one place! Being part of the international writing community! Stars in their eyes, the naïf can only see all their writing dreams coming true. Who knows, they might even come out of this with an agent!

However, a local Worldcon can be a cautionary tale. With anything from 6-10,000 people under one roof, many of them ambitious writers on the rise, you're just another face in the crowd. The kaffeeklatsch with the editor of that seminal book may be full within minutes. The publishers you want to meet are constantly in business meetings. Your favourite author? They're hanging out with foreign friends they never otherwise see. And your dream agent turns out to be an arsehole if he doesn't recognise your name from the bestseller lists.

Even the programme provides limited respite. It's wonderful to see local heroes being guests of honour, panels about regional folktales or books in Scots – and such a large fan community! But just because you're a Scottish writer at a Scottish convention, it doesn't mean it's all about you. The panels that fill up fastest are the ones with authors Scottish fans rarely see, and that means the big names – established, largely white cishet writers from the US who have the publisher support to make it over here. How is our fledgling author with a handful of stories to compete? The local writer goes home dejected, demotivated and overwhelmed. Sometimes there's nothing like an international convention for reminding you how insignificant you are.

Of course, it's perfectly okay not to go to conventions, but this sounds utterly patronising when it's clearly not the case. Headline-grabbing publishing tales are often born from opportunity – "chance meeting leads to agent signing", "contest winner lands six-figure deal". And where better to find author kismet than at a convention, with publishers, agents, editors, authors and more all under one roof? Many of these events encourage new writers to make themselves visible – there are panels that need participants, workshops that need running, and so forth. Be respectful, focus on making connections rather than throwing your manuscript in people's faces, and watch destiny unfold.

The overnight success story has a lot to answer for here. Certainly, conventions can provide networking shortcuts, but they're part of years of making connections and building up a reputation for good stories – years mysteriously missing from the myth of the dream debut. Logically, we know that not every writer can come away from a con with a million bucks in their back pocket – but wouldn't it be great if you could? Look at these wunderkinds, impeccably dressed and smiling, ever alert for the perfect opportunity with that perfect manuscript in hand. If only you could crack the formula! "Fairy tales can come true / It can happen to you…"

All this makes the longing worse. Our profession is public, but the craft is solitary, honed over long hours pouring our heart onto the page. Putting ourselves out there, risking public embarrassment – where's the attraction? *Rejection is just part of the industry*, we're told. *Grow a thick skin. Act professional*. When the very nature of what you do is personal, it's hard to take it otherwise. Yet we go to events time and time again, because it's the easiest way to engage with the industry. A writer's dilemma is not so much *is it okay to not go to a convention*, more *can you afford to miss this?* And after a while, *how much more of this can I take?*

If these feelings fester, conventions stop being a place where you feel like part of a community of fans and creatives. Quite the opposite. Your peers are your competition in a race to capture lightning in a bottle. You can't risk missing your golden opportunity. Add in the success stories and the inevitable pressure to replicate them, it's a recipe for self-loathing, jealousy, and cut-throat behaviour. Like publishing's own real-life Hunger Games, it's the hope that kills.

My own motivations have been on my mind recently, albeit initially for different reasons. Lockdown for my family never really ended, with my father's terminal respiratory illness reaching the inevitable end last Autumn and mortality having its way with several other relatives. Though none of this was really unexpected, its impact has been: while I thought I should be getting out into the world again (for my own mental health as much as dearly-missed friends), I felt myself reaching for those excuses I thought I'd long since put away with much of my social anxiety. I didn't feel ready to attend conventions again, a good enough reason on its own, but I couldn't help thinking there was something else going on.

This changed last November, when I escaped to Edinburgh for the inaugural Cymera Writers Conference. I figured I could claim this as training for my PhD, as an event aimed at early career writers. However the first talk of the day was from Marcus Gipps, Publishing Director of Gollancz's SF Masterworks series: a curiosity in the programme considering Masterworks only publishes works at least 20 years old. However, during his hour onstage, Marcus expressed something that I'd been feeling for a while but hadn't been able to articulate.

He asked a question – what is it that makes these ascribed classics of the genre last? Certainly, for the Masterworks series, there was what you'd hope for from any book – entertaining in terms of plot, characterisation and prose. However, Marcus listed other possible features, such as extrapolation from the present, originality in worldbuilding, contribution to ongoing conversations in genre, and thought-provoking in terms of life or culture. While I don't necessarily agree that all of these make for great works of literature (prediction in particular), the overall sense of them – interesting, groundbreaking, influential or ahead of their time – felt right to me. In essence, they were simply good books, whatever the reason for that might be.

This was a bolt of lightning for me. I thought of my favourite books from when I was younger, before every novel I read was as much a lesson in current trends or in the craft as they were entertainment. The books I loved and admired, dog-eared from months in the bottom of my schoolbag, all had a something I still hadn't really grasped. I could certainly go back and analyse plot, prose, characterisation, but it was more about what these formed altogether. An atmosphere, a feeling. I remembered what started me writing in the first place – wanting to write stories like these. Feeling like I *could* write books like these.

And then I realised what was missing.

I hadn't connected my thoughts about storytelling to my issues with events. Indeed, I'd deliberately separated them, since for me the need to promote myself conflicts with a writing practice that requires me to get out of my own way, so to speak. But in doing so, I'd committed a fundamental error: conventions for me had become purely about self-promotion, not about craft, Science Fiction and Fantasy, or the other things I loved about being there. Specifically, it was the form of self-promotion that requires you to be constantly performing, ever-vigilant for those golden opportunities. And right then, this didn't hold any attraction for me.

I realised that if I was going to make decisions about anything even remotely writing-related, and that I wanted these decisions to be good for me, I needed to rediscover my motivation for being a writer and use that as my guide. What I should and shouldn't be doing as an early career writer, forever looking for the next opportunity, was simply no good to me anymore. Perhaps it never really was.

> "I needed to rediscover my motivation for being a writer and use that as my guide."

So, when the next convention loomed, I took a step back. Was it important for my work to be there in person this time? Was it important for *me*? Could I get as much as I needed by being there online instead? In the end, I went for the digital option, and not only got some solid work done on my novel, but also attended an online-only workshop that was specifically relevant to the part I was working on. I missed chances to reconnect with industry colleagues, but would I have really taken advantage of these opportunities if I was worried about the work? I missed my friends, but I knew it was the right decision.

I don't claim this as a panacea for convention stress. I am saying that finding your motivation can help with making decisions. The pressure is off – opportunities are no longer about competing, succeeding or failing, but about what is right for you. Do you need to work, or will a weekend at a convention seeing your writing friends keep you going? Do you want to write a story for that anthology, or would you rather progress your novel? Is this a real opportunity, or just another distraction? Whether your decision works out or not doesn't matter. I took a month in January to work my arse off on a story for my dream anthology – and was rejected. However, that same story sold to another publication on my top ten list. 'Invitation' is due out in *ParSec Magazine* very soon. Even if I'd only come out of it with a story I'm damn proud of, I'd still call that a win.

Crucially, a guiding motivation focusses your mind on the most important part of being a writer – the conjuring of story and what that takes. For that reason, it's worth revisiting your specific priorities every so often. Conventions can feel like a crap shoot – the publishing industry, one giant rigged casino. But if you let your own motivation be your guide, the odds will always be in your favour.

Ruth EJ Booth is a multiple award-winning writer and academic of fantasy based in Glasgow, Scotland. Her poetry and fiction can be found in Black Static, Pseudopod and The Dark magazine, as well as anthologies from NewCon Press and Fox Spirit Books. Winner of the BSFA Award for Best Short Fiction and shortlisted twice for the British Fantasy Award in the same category, in 2018 she received an honorable mention for Ellen Datlow's Best Horror of the Year, Volume 10. In 2019, her quarterly column for Shoreline of Infinity, 'Noise and Sparks', received the British Fantasy Award for Best Non-Fiction.

Science Fiction, Fantasy & Dark Fantasy in Fiction and Academia.

Luna Press PUBLISHING

Academia Lunare LUNA PRESS PUBLISHING

Award Winning Scottish Independent Press
Est. 2015
www.lunapresspublishing.com

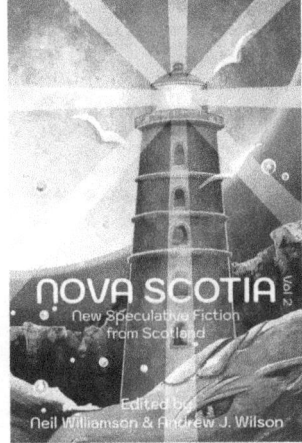

THE UTOPIA OF US
An anthology inspired by Yevgeny Zamyatin's *We*
Edited by Teika Marija Smits

ANNE CHARNOCK • RAYN EPREMIAN • R.T. ESTER
LIAM HOGAN • TIM MAJOR • NADYA MERCIK
FIONA MOSSMAN • ANNA ORRIDGE • SOFIA SAMATAR
ANA SUN • ADRIAN TCHAIKOVSKY • MICHAEL TEASDALE
DOUGLAS THOMPSON • IAN WHATES • ALIYA WHITELEY

NOVA SCOTIA Vol 2
New Speculative Fiction from Scotland
Edited by Neil Williamson & Andrew J. Wilson

DAKINI ATOLL
'The love child of *Akiro* and *Gravity's Rainbow*' Steven Shaviro
NIKHIL SINGH
'African writing at its finest' Mame Bougouma Diene, Caine Prize Winner

TIFFANI ANGUS / VAL NOLAN
SPEC FIC FOR NEWBIES Vol. 2
A Beginner's Guide to Writing More Subgenres of Science Fiction, Fantasy, and Horror

THE INVISIBLE GIRL
CL FARLEY

TANGLEWOOD
KNICKY L ABBOTT

THE LAST TO DROWN
LORRAINE WILSON

SWAN KNIGHT
FUMIO TAKANO
Translated by Shami Wilson

- **JOHN'S EYES** — JOANNA CORRANCE
- **JUST ADD WATER** — JOHN DODD
- **DREAD BROKEN WITCH** — ANDREW WALLACE
- **FUTURE GOD OF LOVE** — DILMAN DILA
- **SKIN FOR SKIN** — TERRY GRIMWOOD
- **CLOCKWORK SISTER** — M E RODMAN

- **HOVERING** — DOROTHY-JANE DANIELS
- **A FACE IN THE LEAVES** — NINA ORAM
- **MOMENT TO REMEMBER, FORGET** — TIFFANY JIMENEZ
- **THE CHANCELS OF MAINZ** — RUSSELL HEMMELL
- **LUCA** — OR LUCA
- **THE QUEEN OF THE HIGH FIELDS** — RHIANNON A GRIST

- **BROKEN PARADISE** — EUGEN BACON
- **ASHES OF THE ANCESTORS** — ANDREW KNIGHTON
- **THE NIGHT BEGINS** — ABIGAIL F TAYLOR
- **MIASMA** — JESS HYSLOP
- **THE LIES WE TELL OURSELVES** — LK KITNEY
- **VIRGIN LAND** — CHLOE SMITH

SCIENCE FICTION AND ABOLISHING THE POLICE

S. J. Groenewegen

Ursula Le Guin. Photo by Marian Wood Kolisch

In 2014, Ursula K. Le Guin gave a short speech when accepting the USA's National Book Foundation Medal for Distinguished Contribution to American Letters. These four sentences resonate ten years on:

"We live in capitalism, its power seems inescapable — but then, so did the divine right of kings. Any human power can be resisted and changed by human beings. Resistance and change often begin in art. Very often in our art, the art of words."

Science fiction is ideal for exploring just how we humans

can resist and change the power structures we create. We can and should use science fiction stories to imagine and test better futures, and how we might arrive there. Policing is one social structure ripe for science fictional re-imaginings.

The police are among the most powerful civilian institutions in representative democracies. While specifics differ between jurisdictions, the common police functions are to detect and solve crime, enforce the law and prevent disorder. Police are an integral part of the criminal justice system where rule of law is a governing principle. Unlike private detectives and private security, police are agents of the state even where they operate with political independence. Guarding against the abuse of police powers is vital, albeit too often lacking.

Police appear in science fiction stories across all media. It's difficult to identify the first time a cop appeared in a science fiction tale, but according to Mark Cole in *Clarkesworld*, that honour might belong to Hal Clement's *Needle*, first serialised in *Astounding Science Fiction* during 1949. In that novel, an alien symbiote is effectively a cop pursuing a fugitive.

But if there's one story that's left a genre-blurring legacy, it would be Isaac Asimov's *The Caves of Steel*, first serialised in *Galaxy Magazine* during 1953. Elijah Baley and R. Daneel Olivaw are police detectives, one human and the other a robot. That set-up of odd-couple cop-buddies solving crimes is now far from being a rarity in science fiction.

Policing is more than solving crime. Enforcing the law and preventing disorder are foundational features, evolving from the origin stories of civilian police organisations worldwide. Not that the history is a long one; the first consistent and disciplined police organisation started in London in 1829 and the Metropolitan Police became the template of civilian police organisations around the world, including the USA. However, the impact of patrols hunting runaway slaves in southern states of the USA and the military taking on policing duties in Britain's colonies cannot be ignored when looking at how modern police operate.

Science fiction doesn't ignore these aspects of policing. Deckard and his fellow replicant hunters in Philip K. Dick's *Do Androids Dream of Electric Sheep* (1968) and in the *Bladerunner* films (1982, 2017) are reminiscent of the slave patrols. Dick's story is also seminal in the science fictional take on noir detective stories. That influence can be seen in a variety of works, including *Star Cops* (BBC, 1987), the cyberpunk Japanoir novel *Tea from an Empty Cup* (1998) by Pat Cadigan, Detective Miller in *The Expanse* series by James S. A. Corey (2011-2024), among many others.

Finding people is a core skill for police; not only suspected criminals, but missing kids. That crosses into community policing, where police officers are meant to be trustworthy, the people to go to when help is needed, like children lost in crowded places. It's what makes the appropriation of a Los Angeles Police Department uniform by the T-1000 in *Terminator 2: Judgment Day* (1991) particularly chilling as he searches for the young John Connor. As if to punctuate the point, the T-1000 stabs John's foster father through a milk carton. From the mid-1980s to the mid-1990s, milk cartons were used in the USA to publicise missing children with dubious results.

Actual cops going bad happen often enough to highlight how much power police hold over fellow citizens. The FBI observed that serial killers often desire to work in law enforcement, and in several cases succeeded in committing horrific crimes while serving as police officers. *Mad Max* (1979) shows a twist on that reality by depicting the consequences of societal brutality when road cop Max chooses violent retribution.

More common are corrupt police officers. Police corruption is explored in several science fiction stories. They include the 2002 film version of Philip K. Dick's 1956 novella *The Minority Report*, *Person of Interest* (2011-2016) and *The Equalizer* (2021-ongoing). As with the standard police procedural series, hero cops are often pitched against a rotten few.

Dystopian science fiction often features walls of militaristic police in their role of "maintaining the peace". In the USA, Special Weapons and Tactics (SWAT) teams were introduced during the politically turbulent 1960s. Their numbers grew in the decades since, and their use of military-style equipment and uniforms define them. Most, if not all, civilian police organisations worldwide have similar units. The original *2000AD* comic strips about Judge Dredd from 1977 is the epitome of envisaged future cops stomping around in boots and body-armour and acting as cop, judge and executioner. *RoboCop* (1987) is another satirical dystopian tale of militarised policing. The distinction between militarised civilian anti-riot cops and the military is often blurred in the recent rush of dystopian YA novels and their movie adaptations, and in numerous *Doctor Who* episodes.

ACAB, "defund the police" and "abolish the police" are rallying cries against real-world police brutality. On the present trajectory in many countries, these calls are largely ignored by those in power. The status quo seems inescapable.

In contrast, science fiction has a long history of stories showing worlds with no need for police or carceral criminal justice systems. Le Guin wrote a fair few of them but is far from alone.

What's missing are the bridging stories that show how we could get from dystopian now to those utopian futures. How might the systems encouraging police thuggery be dismantled without inadvertently causing worse issues? It is time for science fiction to show us possibilities in resisting the apparently inevitable march to dystopian militarised policing and change how law enforcement works. To go beyond unheeded warnings to something new, something better for all..

Born and raised in Australia, **S. J. Groenewegen** has written numerous SFF essays, short stories and novels, most recently The Disinformation War (GoldSF, 2023). She often appears at SFF conventions as a panellist and moderator. Her former career was in law enforcement and criminal justice, mostly in intelligence analysis, and she worked with Australian law enforcement agencies as well as the UK's National Crime Agency, the Dutch Police, and the FBI. In 2016 she was awarded a British Empire Medal (Civil Division) for services to law enforcement and LGBTQIA diversity. She now lives in the Scottish Highlands.

INTER

Bram E. Gieben

A Q&A with Pippa Goldschmidt

> **Bram E. Gieben** (Glasgow) has written about music, film, TV and comics for Sublation Magazine, The Quietus, io9, Mishka NYC and other places. He hosts the philosophical podcast Strange Exiles.
>
> The 2015 Scottish Slam Poetry Champion, Bram has performed his work at venues and festivals worldwide, from the Edinburgh Fringe and Hidden Door festivals to New York's NuYorican Cafe, and The Kerouac Effect in New Zealand.
>
> Bram's most recent book, *The Darkest Timeline* (published by Revol Press), issues nine theoretical vignettes of doom that trace the outlines of our dystopian present, and our increasingly impossible futures. Russell Jones' review of The Darkest Timeline for Shoreline is on pagepage 120.
>
> This is a shortened version of the full interview which can be found at
>
> www.shorelineofinfinity.com/qa-with-bram-e-gieben/.

1. Can you introduce your book to us?

The book is grounded in the politics, aesthetics and worldview of cyberpunk, much like the music I make. I'm exploring the same themes of surveillance, corporate control, ecological anxiety and technological acceleration, but this time through the lens of critical theory. I analyse the work of cyberpunk authors like William Gibson using the ideas of Mark Fisher, the critic who popularised the saying: 'It's easier to imagine the end of the world than the end of capitalism.' In many ways, this is where the book begins.

Great thinkers like Fisher, John Gray, Slavoj Žižek and others all have things to say about our increasingly precarious future as a culture, and our dystopian present. I use their theories to explore and criticise popular and lesser-known dystopias from fiction, film, video games and TV.

I look at some of the hard science behind climate collapse and drone technology, and explore thought experiments like Fermi's Paradox and Nick Bostrom's 'Simulation argument' to see what they can tell us about the near future, and the choices we have left to make.

In the TV show 'Community', the darkest timeline begins when a character rolls a die. I think we live in a similar moment. I hope the book is a timely reflection on some of the dangers we face, and the hope we need to find in order to face them without flinching.

2. Science fiction's power lies in its ability to articulate and critique those futures, and here you deliberately foreground the ones as conceptualised by cyberpunk. Could you say a bit more about why you chose this particular subgenre?

I was born in 1980, and

cyberpunk imagery and themes dominated the culture I consumed as a teenager. So cyberpunk is our literature, the literature of those trying to conceptualise what a world shaped by these technologies might look like. At the same time, concepts from cyberpunk have inspired, predicted, and continue to predict the evolution of these technologies. I like to remember that William Gibson typed his description of the internet as a "consensual hallucination" on a 1927 Hermes portable typewriter. He was a visionary, as were figures like Bruce Sterling and John Shirley, or K.W. Jeter.

I believe any science fiction that doesn't deal with the foreshortened distance between an unrecognisably techno-augmented society and our deeply unequal, hypercapitalist present is just escapist fantasy. So-called 'post-cyberpunk' genres like Solarpunk, Biopunk or Retro-futurism feel like regressive call backs to an era when SF writers imagined the future as a place of optimism, hope and adventure. Cyberpunk is the inheritor of a darker SF tradition that includes Brunner, Philip K. Dick, George Orwell and Stanislaw Lem, among others - writers who deal with psychology, consciousness, control, and the intersection of humanity and technology. I don't think of cyberpunk as the 'best' genre of modern SF. I consider it the only genre.

BRAM E GIEBEN

THE DARKEST TIMELINE

Living in a World with No Future

3. *Imagining the apocalypse is not a new pastime, it seems to go hand-in-hand with a developing human consciousness. And perhaps the end of the world is not only happening now, but has always been happening – every historical era has its wars, famines, plagues etc.We are always building on the ashes of previous destruction. Or am I wrong in trying to preserve some sense of optimism?*

You're right to say that each generation, era and culture has its own version of the 'end times' myth, and that every previous generation has faced down some sort of existential threat or millenarian fear. I think that comes in large part from our inheritance of the Judaeo-Christian apocalypse tradition, but also from the teleological nature of Christian cosmology itself. All the stories we tell have one eye on the future, and on some form of redemption. A better world to come, but only after a time of judgement and violence.

The key issue about which I have very little optimism is far more important and dangerous than questions of growth, technological threats, or climate collapse. That issue is inequality. We in the West have very high living standards. Bringing the rest of the world up to a similar standard - including the enormous carbon cost of our consumption - would likely exceed the world's ability to produce resources, and rapidly accelerate the speed of climate collapse.

To propose that instead we should all embrace a strategy like degrowth - where our quality of life decreases (as measured by neoliberal standards), and we travel less, consume less and fundamentally need less - seems no less idealistic or unlikely. We're all very used to fast cars, fast food, fast fashion. I think most people are cautiously hoping that technology will save us, but as I explore in the book, this is a shaky peg on which to hang our hopes.

A great many people understandably see this as someone else's problem. They're not wrong. It will be our descendants who deal with the most disastrous consequences of the choices we make now, and the choices we fail to make. On the evidence so far, the will to do something just isn't there.

What does this mean for hope? I try and cover this in the last chapter. I think turning away from statistical prediction and capitalist solution-engineering is one way to gain back a feeling of personal agency when it comes to these questions. Look instead for what you can do locally, or even just in your family home, to live in ways which are more in tune with the natural world; less oriented around technology, and more focused on human interaction. I'm not necessarily saying that solutions can be found there. But even if the worst happens, these are the places where we'll try to survive, and the people we'll do our best to save. One reason the world feels so apocalyptic now is that we bear witness to so many crises, atrocities and catastrophes. These have always been present, but now they are ever-present, and often we're powerless to do much besides watch. I find hope much harder to sustain in the face of issues I can't affect or solve, and which happen at a distance. I think focusing on what you can affect, and who you can help, is a valid response to those feelings. That's one of the reasons I wrote the book! We can't change what we won't face.

AI Candy

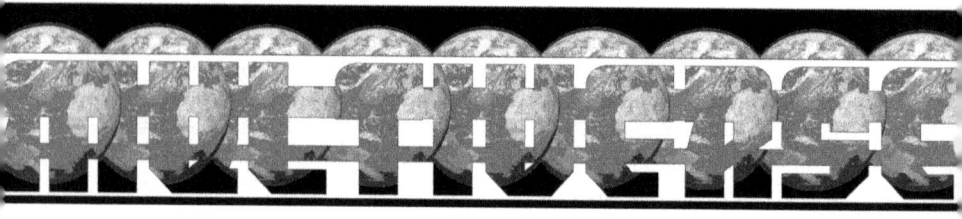

Anna Cheung

It arrived in a coffin-like box
marked *fragile*. I signed for It.

In the dim bedroom, I unpeeled
the cardboard, revealed Its beigeness

revealed the large hands, manicured.
The smoothness resembled skin.

I found the sweet spot, turned It on.
It became He, unfolded rubber flesh

unfolded muteness to reveal a GSOH.
He said it was great to meet me F2F,

but had to set the record straight,
by correcting some misconceptions

(NB was non-binary, not *nota bene*)

They ask if I wanted NSA or LTR
I was confused. *Just touch me. Please.*
So, they educated me on GGG

as they pressed my...oh oh *oh*...

Nocturnal

Anna Cheung

The radio station reports 63°C.
Oceans spit out marine bones,
tides churn like hot soup.
We stay indoors; blinds shuttered.

Night is cool yet moonless.
We emerge as pale sick creatures
thirsting for the moist darkness.
Our tongues quench on shadows.

I fear to prise the slats apart.
My eyes are radiation burns,
the giant star a scar on my mind.
My brain becomes a black hole

sucking at the bones of the carcass
landscape and broken charcoal limbs.

Anna Cheung is a poet based in Glasgow. Her debut poetry collection entitled *Where Decay Sleeps* was published by Haunt Publishing. Amongst other writings, her previous works were published in the anthologies *Golden Hours, Haunted Voices, Forward Book of Poetry* and literary magazines such as *The Dark Horse, Myth & Lore, Banshee Journal, Dreich* and *Zarf*. She was highly commended by the Forward Prize in 2022.

She has performed at various spoken word events including Cymera Festival, Granite Noir, Edinburgh Literary Salon and Edinburgh Book Festival.

Fibonacci Poem for the James Webb Space Telescope
Jeda Pearl

—

space

time

rotates

hypnotic

phyllotactical

branching into prehistory

so deep it's almost unfathomable to us specks.

Earth-clamped, in awe of unravelling galaxies, we are momentarily undone.

Worlds upon worlds contained in a single grain of sand — how can this universe be finite? We follow a chameleon's tail, ammonite,

conch shell, pine cone, fern unfurling, wave cresting, whirlpool, slow wine, heart beat. Irrational yet intuitive flows, releasing seismic change, reactional heat vortexes in the vast void, luscious dark energy is inscrutable.

We collect photons, claiming them as they redshift, pouring through time to those early, wondrous years. Momentous travelling, eons of light-years, as if an actual moment of light is that simple. What did they have to pass through to reach us? Fragments fragmenting into golden ratios, reflected on beryllium mirrors, beamed back to multicellular mites.

Hosting galaxies within, our fibonacci branches of DNA pattern curls of life. Stardust-formed, we bathe in golden sun, seeking stars' spectra outwith our milk-dust spiral playground. Even hurricanes look beautiful from the moon. We cannot stay — our sun will eat our blue home. Galaxies undone, neutrinos guide us through chaos, teach us how to shape-shift. In earthships with spectrogram portholes, textured reliefs on panelled walls whispering wonders, our rods and cones upgraded to witness imperceptible transitions into theoretical dimensions we can't yet quite comprehend.

Time Cleaves Itself

Jeda Pearl

Space and Time collided when planning this issue's Multiverse. At exactly that moment Jeda Pearl sent out an email announcing the publication of her debut collection which arrived in my email inbox.

I've followed Jeda's progress over recent years, at various events such as 'Figures of Speech –Future, at the Storytelling Centre' [1] where she performed a vibrant and inspiring piece called *Caledonian Forest, 3033*

Time Cleaves Itself is published by Peepal Tree Press
Book cover design by Kezia Lewis @studio.kezikoko

 And as one of the perks of booking acts for our Event Horizon, I've always been delighted when Jeda accepted our invitations to perform.

So when the message from Jeda arrived, it was a matter of seconds to reply to ask if we could publish some of her poems from _Time Cleaves Itself_ in this issue of Shoreline. Jeda said yes.

I haven't read the collection yet, but after reading the poems she sent me, I cannot wait. Read *Fibonacci Poem for the James Webb Space Telescope* and marvel at the power of the imagery as it unfurls explosively from a dot to encompass the whole universe. And describes the workings of Jame Webb works in passing. Why is observational astronomy so important? This piece tells you why, and I hope is read by anyone interested in taking up astronomy.

In her email Jeda tells me: "there are several fantastical, sci-fi and science-inspired poems in the collection, but also poems on nature, disability, illness, growing up and being a person of colour in Scotland, and ones that swim between and combine those themes!"

Even more reason to dive in to *Time Cleaves Itself*, it seems to me.

—Noel Chidwick

---

[1] watch the video at https://jedapearl.com/figures-of-speech-future/

Reform: Gate 42

Jeda Pearl

We meet and will meet and have already met
astride the pintuck of event horizon
unravelling the neutrino gate
reconstructing
reweaving
:
They
try to cram us
inower thair tapestries
claucht in fragmented parallel worlds
but we can translate one another's particles
and they are bone scared, suspecting the silence
is alive, as the youtdem untangle decaying strands
from overbrimming dark matter

Jeda Pearl is a Scottish Jamaican writer. In 2022, she was shortlisted for the Sky Arts RSL Award in poetry and longlisted for the Women Poets' Prize. Her poems appear in art installations and several anthologies, and her debut poetry collection, Time Cleaves Itself, is published by Peepal Tree Press. @JedaPearl / jedapearl.com

Courie-in tae th Dark

Jeda Pearl

Wrap yersel in midnicht
Fauld-in moon-lickit whisker clouds
Crease Winter's solstice tae Beltane's dew
and kiss Midsummer's bountiful last licht

Drape Samhuinn's lively dusk ower heid and shoulder
Daunder on th slopes o heaven
Glide unner th glut o noctilucent nimbus

Courie-in tae th nae-knawin
Swing and dive intae undulatin mysteries
Sky, alive and divine, reflects yer dark matter back
It's okay you dinnae ken whit's gwan

Slip intae th eastern sunset
Swaddle yer mortality in nocturnal sustenance
Drink in th milk o dyin starlight
Th harmonies o th spheres are waitin

Wash yer face in cosmic gloam
Reminisce tae th throbbin dawin
Knit spindrifts o departin dark
and sleep, sated and cleansed, until morn

I owe a depth of thanks to Noel Chidwick, Russell Jones, Rachel Plummer and the Shoreline of Infinity community!

I would not have explored poetry so fully without their support. The very first two poems I had published was in the Multiverse anthology – this early encouragement and recognition was fundamental to my life and career as a poet and their ongoing support has really meant the world to me

—Jeda Pearl

REVIEWS

Catch-up

Umbilical
Teika Marija Smith
Published by NewCon Press in August 2023
Review by Elizabeth Ryder

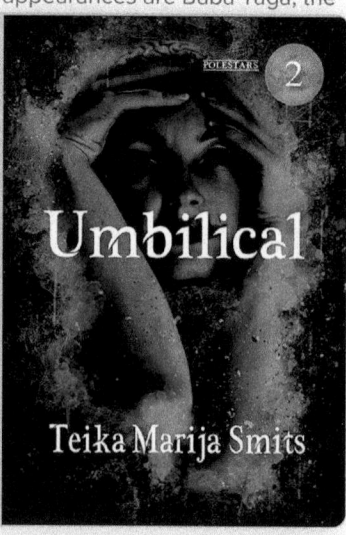

Teika Marija Smits' short story collection *Umbilical* could just as easily have been titled *Labyrinthian*, as much for its twisting, maze-like structure as for its frequent references to the myth of Theseus and the Minotaur. Also making guest appearances are Baba Yaga, the Green Man, Bluebeard, Sherlock Holmes and Chernila— the latter being a goddess of stories and poetry who seems to the author's own invention. Each story in the collection can be read as a standalone, but small details here and there suggest that several are, tantalizingly, interlinked. The coffee-shop AI in 'Death of the Grapevine' describes a conversation between a writer and a woman who has read her book, the other side of which is recounted several stories later in 'A Piece of Fabric The Size of a Pin'. In 'How to Honour a Beginning', the Green Man of folklore, newly arrived on Earth, wonders "which species would be so cruel, so *stupid*, to rid a planet of trees?" His question appears to be answered in 'The Green Man', in which a group of young people attend a Green Man festival as a break from the drudgery of their dystopian, fully urbanised society. Baba Yaga, meanwhile, appears in 'Beginning', alongside Chernila (who also makes an appearance in 'Size of a Pin' and 'Grapevine'), and the Siren, as the crone part of the Maiden, Mother, Crone triptych. She then pops up again in 'ATU339 the Wise' (one of my personal favourites), circling a black hole and setting her riddles and impossible tasks to an adventurous AI, the troublesome humans having lost interest in her after the invention of space travel. Artificial intelligences, fairytales, Greek myths and dystopian futures are interwoven throughout this anthology. In 'Minotaur/Mindtour' a futuristic Theseus must travel through a mental labyrinth to overthrow the evil king of an interstellar empire. In *Machina in Deo* a group of sapient machines contemplate their own divinity. In 'A Survival Guide for the Contemporary Princess' the titular princess is not a princess at all, but a mafia wife whose 'prince' is the android guardian assigned to her by a witness protection program. Motherhood is another theme that permeates the collection, although not quite as much as the title would suggest. 'Umbilical', the story that lends the collection its name, is one of the strangest, describing the physical *regrowth* of the umbilical chord between a mother and daughter as the former supports the latter through a terminal cancer diagnosis. It's a poignant image, but the practicalities at times border on the ridiculous: "Try not to freak out about it," the daughter says, "but I have this, like, weird chord thing growing out of my belly button." "I've got one too," her mother confesses. "Coming out of my, well... fanny."'His Birth' is another strange one. On the outset, it's a simple enough story about a woman having to choose between taking a painkiller that may cause infertility or living with pain and clinging to her hope of having a child. The painkiller in question, though, isn't a drug but rather a giant fish-like creature that sucks on the affected body part like a leech. (This story also features some pretty extreme medical self-harm, which squeamish readers may want to skip.)The story that most missed the mark for me was 'Our Lady of Flies', about a teacher who is caught by her husband, *in flagrante* with one of her former students. Although everyone in the story is over the age of eighteen, the sex scene between the two of them is still somewhat uncomfortable to read, especially as the level of detail given borders on the pornographic. My main issue with the story, though, is that after that climactic scene we somehow have over eleven pages still to go, during which nothing much happens. 'Flies' has the distinction of being both one of the longest stories in the anthology, and one of the least eventful.For most of the stories in *Umbilical*, the shorter they are, the better they work. 'ATU339 the Wise' and 'Girl's Night Out' (seemingly a typical story of a group of women going out for drinks, but with an unexpected dramatic twist), are just under two and five pages respectively, and yet are two of the best sci-fi stories in the bunch.The exceptions to this rule are 'The Case of the High Pavement Ghosts', 'The Eyes of the Goddess Herself', and 'The November Room (or

Leaving the Labyrinth)' all three of which benefit from a longer length that allows Smits to properly stretch her imaginative wings.'Ghosts' tells the tale of Sherlock Holmes's ghost-hunting female cousin, who is summoned by the detective when one of his cases starts to show elements of the supernatural. The characters in this story and the set-up of the central mystery are compelling, and the ghosts themselves a chilling presence. Unfortunately, the ending does fall off a bit (in fairness, a failing that it shares with a fair few of the Conan Doyle originals). 'Eyes' is an otherworldly fable about a young woman whose artistic talent provokes supernatural sabotage by a jealous husband. This story is probably the one that benefits most from the extra space, allowing the author to weave a compelling mythology around the world her protagonist lives in.'November Room' is the final story, and the spiritual, if not literal, sequel to 'Minotaur/Mindtour', featuring a woman trapped in a mysterious labyrinth that forces her to relive various moments from her life in the aftermath of a great personal tragedy. This story's strength comes in its piecemeal revelation of the facts via a series of flashbacks, and the extra length allows it to do this to great effect. *Umbilical* is a labyrinth that lures the reader in and tempts them to find its centre. Explorers are advised to look out for minotaurs, and to leave a tangle of yarn behind them, lest they lose their way in the dark.

The Darkest Timeline

Bram E. Gieben

Published by Revol Press in June 2024

Review by Russell Jones

Whether it's death by meteorite, being eaten alive by a zombie horde or just a particularly hot day with a distinct lack of ice cream to cool down, most of us have thought about the end of the world. Humanity's doom – lovingly referred to as The Apocalypse – is the focus of *The Darkest Timeline*, a new collection of non-fiction essays by writer and musician Bram E Gieben.

The book is short but substantial, covering some of the literary precedence for apocalyptic narratives, and delving into the potential major causes of humankind's downfall. These include robotic drones, virtual realities, the climate crisis, surveillance technologies and plenty more. It's a veritable smorgasbord of chilling possibilities and, unusually, I would recommend that anybody on the brink of bad thoughts may want to wait until their horizons seem perkier before opening these pages. Gieben doesn't pull any punches, often stating outright that – to paraphrase – we're probably already screwed in multiple ways. The apocalypse isn't just an idea, a fantasy or a possibility in the far future... it's already here.

That's not to say that the book is entirely pessimistic about the future of the species, but pessimism (or perhaps the author would call it "realism") is winning with odds approximately 99:1. As something of an eternal optimist myself, I felt a certain sense of impending dread as I began, but was reassured by the introduction's promise that, "we cannot give into absolute pessimism". A glint of hope, then. And sometimes all I need is a glint.

Shoreline of Infinity readers, or indeed any fans of excellent SF, will likely be wondering in what ways these essays might intersect with Science Fiction. Gieben has done his homework, pulling in examples from classic and modern SF texts, movies, video games and other cultural artifacts for those with a (potentially unhealthy, go to the clinic!) piqued interest in oblivion. These include *Star Trek, The Matrix, Call of Duty: Black Ops, Pokemon GO, Neuromancer, Foundation* and many many more. Gieben provides brief summaries for most, so those references aren't lost on the uninitiated. He goes into much greater details with some resources, such as John Barnes' *Kaleidoscope Century*. The author also provides a substantial bibliography, which will act as a fantastic resource for anyone wishing to continue their voyage of the damned.

The Darkest Timeline considers apocalyptic beginnings as imagined in SF, and explores how those medias have shaped our consciousnesses around The End. It turns out that they have not always been helpful because they often imagine us as underdogs and heroes winning against the odds, rather than simply succumbing to mankind's decline powerlessly (which is likely more realistic). A sugar-coated pill against reality, if you will, although this isn't always the case and Gieben offers up many useful examples to the contrary. On these introductory segments, however, I think it would have been of great benefit for Gieben to establish more of a sense of *why* apocalypse narratives are so ingrained in human consciousness and culture, before continuing to address how they have been adapted or commodified in modern society. There seems a psychological and sociological element that could be teased out to add this framework, mainly so that I/the reader can better understand the context and history of the modernisation. Did cavemen worry about the apocalypse? Did the Victorians? Surely, yes. But at least the Victorians had cake to alleviate the concern.

There were many things to admire about *The Darkest Timeline*, not least the occasional snippet of humour to lighten the mood. At least, I think it was humour (I'm not always the best at identifying a joke) and I laughed. This one made me chuckle: "conservative self-help salesman Jordan Peterson" (p11). This occasional humour helps the whole text from feeling dry or overly academic (like a mathematician in the Gobi), and this is further helped by the author's blending of poetic or musical language. There's a certain beauty to the way that Gieben describes the end times, and it comes as no surprise given he's an accomplished rap artist / musician (I don't know what the preferred title is these days. I really should go back to a music festival, it's been decades now. But the toilets...) Here are some of my favourite examples of Gieben's creative palette adding colour to the canvas:

"The cost of civilization is measured in poisoned oceans, skeleton coasts and cornfield tundras. It leaks catastrophically, spewing out bubonic ice and rolling death smog." (p21)

"This is the capitalist megachurch, the city-as-mall. You wander down streets thronged with busy foot traffic. A few trees are segmented into boxed planters, drought-stricken islands landlocked in a sea of uniform paving stones." (p87)

"This is the future of our inner cities unless we fight it. The low winter sun colors the anonymous skyscrapers a dull, dusty pink. In the reflective glass, you see only the shadows of the eldritch horrors these nowhere places conceal." (p93)

This aptitude for imaginative description and brevity in storytelling really helped to sell the essays for me. It added nuance and intrigue, alongside statistics and references. Even from the short samples above, I think it's obvious that Gieben is a great storyteller. Indeed the collection builds with each passing chapter, guiding the reader through a series of accounts as to why we are unlikely to wake up to a utopia (if we wake up at all), evoking that unnerving chill that we're meant to feel when someone's walked over our grave. Note: if you do walk over my grave, please remove any weeds. Thanks.

It's not all nukes and roses, though. While Gieben generally gives a good overview of existing arguments and ideas, with well-selected sources which demonstrate an excellent understanding and awareness of the topics he's covering, he has a tendency to make grand-sounding proclamations which I sometimes felt needed a deeper dive to be truly convincing. The author is clearly passionate and (not unduly) angry/sad about the state of the world, but can allow bold and sweeping statements to slide too easily through the metal detector. Some statements are explosive but brief, some concepts are presented as absolutes, and I was left wanting more – either to satisfy my curiosity, or to more fully accept what I was being told. Let's look at a couple of those:

On discussing the positive outlook of Jimmy Carter following the launch of the Voyager probe, Gieben writes: "In the asymmetrical post-apocalyptic society we inhabit today, such a future is in reality radically unthinkable, yet we nonetheless still fervently, naively anticipate it." (p7) Do we? And why is it unthinkable? Perhaps it's simply a misuse of the "we" here, but such statements aren't uncommon and I found myself, at least in part, disagreeing.

Later, Gieben asserts: "Humans will become extinct, as all animals must, and there is no reason to presume that this could not happen in the near term." (p26) I suppose in the entirety of time and space, humankind will one day no longer exist, but *The Darkest Timeline* frequently pushes the narrative that we're already in the process of ultimate destruction. There *are* reasons to presume that this might not happen in the near future, and the author even goes to some (admittedly not huge) lengths to demonstrate this in the final essay, with the entire series ending on this powerful declaration:

"We are storytellers and liars, and we lie to ourselves most often. Perhaps when our distant descendants visit or unearth the libraries that remain, they will be unable to discern lies from stories, science from magic, or records from dusty propaganda. Our descendants could be few, or they could be many. Will they understand what they read? Perhaps not. They may yet find it beautiful, even useful." (p109)

So, even if we die, we live on in the things we leave for the next generation. It's hard to disagree that the apocalypse has occurred if future generations are obliterated along with our own, but there remains that glint of optimism which I mentioned at the start of this review. Although a reader could take this collection as almost entirely pessimistic (I assume the author might call it *realistic*) *The Darkest Timeline* seems to me to come from a position of love, of caring for humanity and the things that truly matter to us: art, community, connection – not consumerism, selfishness or manipulation. Ultimately I took away the message, "if we are to make a better world, we need to understand why and how it is flawed, even if it might be unsavable." (Jones, 2024).

The Darkest Timeline is a brief but excellent collection of essays on the theme of apocalypse. It not only provides its own insights into the much-walked territory of humanity's demise, but will be a great resource for anybody who wishes to continue the journey. Each essay is full of ideas that are worthy of unpacking, and I think it would therefore be an excellent text for anybody interested in pondering or discussing the philosophy of our mortality, as well as many sociological and psychological imperatives set within the environment of the apocalypse. Although I sometimes finished a section unconvinced by its statements, that isn't a damning criticism of this book – Gieben doesn't necessarily *attempt* to convince you of anything, but instead presents ideas and arguments for you to absorb and consider, much like the intelligent sea sponge that you are, right? I appreciate that this book asks questions that it cannot answer. I like that approach, and the fact that it doesn't force feed; like a good teacher, it opens the door and gives you a little shove through it. Unfortunately, outside that open door there might be a mushroom cloud or a swarm of military drones with your face in their databanks. So, good luck, intrepid adventurer!

Mal Goes To War
Edward Ashton

Published by Rebellion Publishing in April 2024

Reviewed by AJ Deane

Mal is a free AI and unconcerned about the war going on between the tech-embracing Federation and the tech-rejecting Humanists. Why should he be worried? He lives in infospace. But his curiosity about physical forms and salvage gets the better of him; he finds himself cut off from infospace, 'puppeting' the body of a mercenary, in a hotly-contested war zone, in the company of the modded (modified) girl the mercenary was protecting. He takes it upon himself to see the girl to the safety of Federation-controlled territory, yet finds himself hamstrung by his reliance on immediate access to infospace, and his lack of connection to those around him. Of course, humans would never do that to themselves... The story which follows is a surprisingly heartwarming exploration of comradeship, duty, honour, and friendship, as a ragtag group, willingly or not, forms around Mal; a very human tale, told from the perspective of a very *in*human protagonist. Or is he?

Machine- or robotic-based intelligences aren't a new thing. *Erewhon* (Samuel Butler) was written in 1872 and we have gone through many iterations since then, both good and bad; Robby the Robot, Hal 9000, Iain M. Banks' Culture series, Data in Star Trek, Rossum's Universal Robots, Metropolis, and so on. However, it is perhaps unsurprising that in the current climate of rapid AI development, Science-Fiction is now producing more stories which feature an AI as the main character, rather than a straightforward enemy. Karl Drinkwater's *Solace* series is another good example of this.

Ashton's is certainly one of the best I've read recently. An all-too believable look at human physical and mental frailty, coupled with the inherent dangers of an artificial intelligence which neither understands that frailty nor, perhaps, wishes to - or worse, which might intend - to exploit it. *Mal Goes to War* is predominantly written in the third person, but there is a level of war or on a personal level, which are the true driving force of the narrative.

The world-building is kept pretty simple, mainly taking place in rural areas and small settlements, and this allows the technical aspects to shine all the brighter; a spark is always more noticeable in the dark. There is more than a little of a cyberpunk leaning; innovative leaps from the wearable tech and military kit which exist in our contemporary lives, to those which could so easily come to be the everyday run-of-the-mill items and implants of the not-too-distant future. This isn't 'Hard SF', though, the tale very much hinges on the interrelationships, and it is in the solidly-written, three-dimensional characters that *Mal Goes to War* excels.

It is also interesting to note that the whole book was very visual. I can totally understand why one of the author's previous novels, *Mickey7*, has been made into a film (*Mickey 17, coming in 2025*); I'll be looking out for that one.

In *Mal Goes To War*, Ashton has created an extremely compelling, very readable satire on what it means to be human, the nature of war, and the future we might make for ourselves.

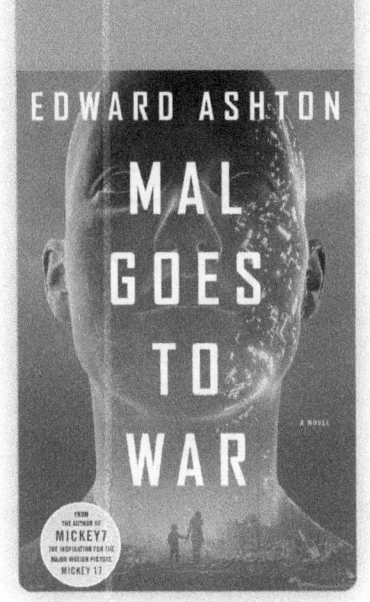

of laconic, wry humour which seems unmistakably Mal's, no doubt helped by the short conversations he has with his friends, Helpdesk and !Clippy. These set the world-weary, or perhaps *human*-weary, tone for the whole book.

Don't let the darkly comedic aspects fool you, this technothriller raises some serious and philosophical questions. Are Artificial Intelligences naturally cynical and slightly sociopathic, by our human terms? Should we use the same points of reference to judge them? What are honour and duty, and who do these serve? Indeed, it's the differences in emotion, intuition, and logic between man and machine, whether in the theatre

Reviews are also published online at
www.shorelineofInfinity.com

SAVE THE DATE FOR

SCOTLAND'S FESTIVAL OF SCIENCE FICTION, FANTASY AND HORROR WRITING

6 - 8 JUNE 2025

IN EDINBURGH AND ONLINE

CYMERA

WWW.CYMERAFESTIVAL.CO.UK

SHORELINE OF INFINITY

Award Winning Science Fiction

Shoreline of Infinity is based in Edinburgh, Scotland, and began life in 2015.

Shoreline of Infinity Science Fiction Magazine is a print and digital magazine published quarterly in PDF, ePub and Kindle formats. It features new short stories, poetry, art, reviews and articles.

But there's more – we run live science fiction events called Event Horizon, with a whole mix of science fiction related entertainments such as story and poetry readings, author talks, music, drama, short films – we've even had sword fighting.

We also publish a range of science fiction related books; take a look at our collection at the Shoreline Shop. You can also pick up back copies of all of our issues. Details on our website...

www.shorelineofinfinity.com

SF CALEDONIA

Wanted:

SF stories by Scottish Writers

What can I submit?

We're looking for stories that have already been published somewhere in the world. Not self-published, or on your own website.

We would love to see contributions in any of the Scottish languages and dialects.

Accepted authors will also be asked to provide a short biography, public contact details (web, social media) and links to where readers can buy their books. This will be posted alongside the story, and be searchable through the website.

Who is a Scottish Writer?

You were born, lived or live in Scotland. The exact criteria are on the website.

Are you looking for help?

SF Caledonia is purely volunteer driven. If you are interested in helping in any capacity, contact the Editor through the website.

Ideas and Suggestions

SF Caledonia is a new model, and we are looking for ideas and suggestions on how to develop it. Do get in touch with your thoughts (especially if you are in a position to help develop your suggestions).

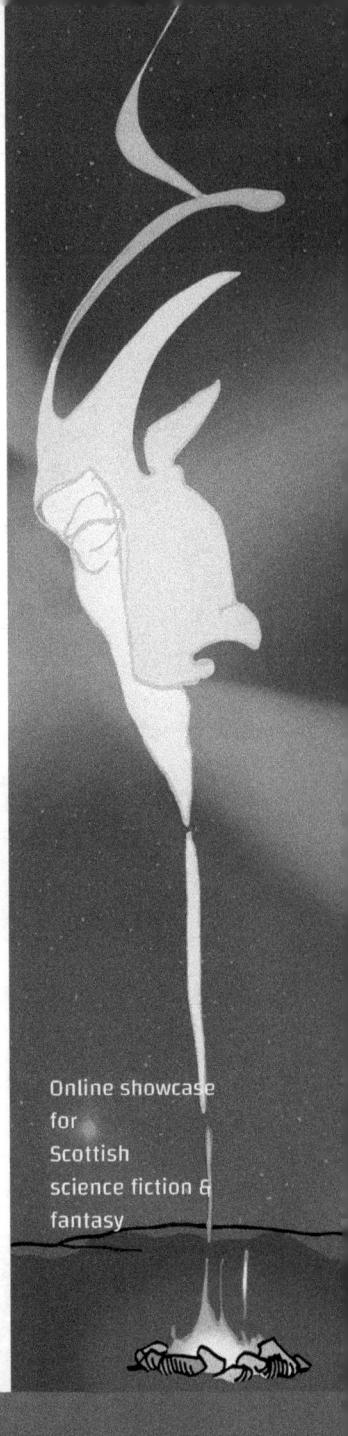

Online showcase for Scottish science fiction & fantasy

www.sfcaledonia.scot

They seem very peaceful and contented. But, occasionally, one grows a couple of extra heads and they fight. After a terrible battle the losing heads are ripped off and it goes back to being calm again.

I'm thinking of naming them "Partipolitix."

Star Draws
Mark Toner